THIS CANDLEWICK BOOK BELONGS TO:

_____

_____

_____

_____

First U.S. paperback edition 1994
The text and illustrations in this book first appeared in
Jack the Carpenter and His Friends, *Jill the Farmer and Her Friends*,
Tom the Greengrocer and His Friends, *Julie the Paper Girl and Her Friends*
all first published in Great Britain by
Walker Books Ltd., London in 1986.

Library of Congress Cataloging-in-Publication Data

Butterworth, Nick.
Busy people / by Nick Butterworth.—1st U.S. ed.
Summary: Introduces the people who work around town and
the equipment they use, including a carpenter, doctor, and grocer.
ISBN 1-56402-056-8 (hardcover)—ISBN 1-56402-365-6 (paperback)
1. Occupations—Juvenile literature. [1. Occupations.] I. Title.
HF5381.2.B88   1992
331.7'02—dc20   91-58719

2 4 6 8 10 9 7 5 3 1

Printed in Hong Kong

The pictures in this book were done in watercolor.

Candlewick Press
2067 Massachusetts Avenue
Cambridge, MA 02140

BUSY PEOPLE

by Nick Butterworth

CANDLEWICK PRESS

CAMBRIDGE, MASSACHUSETTS

Jack is a carpenter.

What does he use?

Anna is a doctor.

Why has she come?

Tom is a grocer.

What does he sell?

Bill is a repairman.

What does he fix?

Jenny is a gardener.

What does she use?

Steve is a fisherman.

What does he sail?

Betty is a baker.

What does she bake?

Jim is a messenger.

What does he ride?

Sally owns a clothing store.

What does she sell?

Dave is a builder.

What does he drive?

Ron has a hardware store.

What does he sell?

Jill is a farmer.

What does she drive?

Pete is a mechanic.

What does he use?

Fred is a garbage collector.

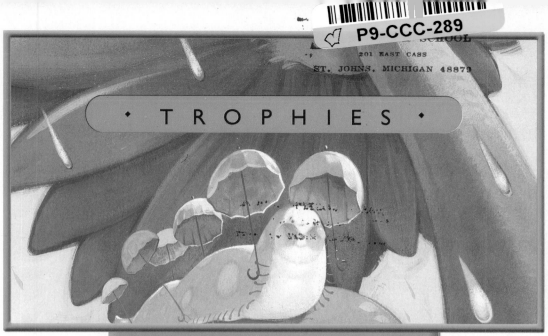

· T R O P H I E S ·

Language Handbook

Grade 2

Printed in the United States of America

ISBN 0-15-325064-X

5 6 7 8 9 10 073 10 09 08 07 06 05 04 03

Orlando   Boston   Dallas   Chicago   San Diego

Visit *The Learning Site!*
www.harcourtschool.com

CONTENTS

Visit *The Learning Site!*
www.harcourtschool.com

Your Best Writing

You can learn a lot about writing just from reading. You can also learn a lot by writing on your own.

This *Language Handbook* can help you learn to write better. It is full of writing models that show you different kinds of writing. It gives you tips to make writing easier.

The Writing Process

Like making a sandwich or painting a picture, writing is an activity that has steps. Many writers use these five steps, or stages.

Prewriting

First, you plan what you are going to write. You might make a list of ideas. You might draw a picture or make a chart.

Drafting

In this stage, you put your ideas in sentences and paragraphs. Follow your prewriting plan as you write a first draft. Do not worry about mistakes.

Revising

In this stage, you reread your draft. You might work with a partner. Talk about your draft, and see how you can make it better.

Proofreading

When you proofread, you check your writing for mistakes, such as missing periods and misspelled words. Then you make a neat final copy.

Publishing

Finally, you choose a way to present your work. You may want to add pictures, make a class book, or read your work aloud.

Keeping a Writer's Journal

A Writer's Journal is a place where you write whatever you want, for fun or practice. It is a good place to keep ideas for writing. You can draw or paste pictures in your journal, too.

To start your journal, choose a notebook. Decorate the cover if you wish. Then fill the pages with your notes and ideas.

You might want to keep a **Word Bank** at the back of your journal. When you find an interesting new word as you read, add it to your Word Bank. Then use some of those words in your writing.

Keeping a Portfolio

A portfolio is a place, such as a folder, to keep your work. You can put your finished pieces of writing in a portfolio. You can show them to your classmates or parents, or you can just enjoy them yourself. You can also get out your portfolio when you meet with your teacher to discuss your writing.

Writer's Craft and Writing Traits

You can play a game if you know the rules. But to play the game well, you have to do more. You have to learn skills and strategies, such as how to aim a basketball so it goes through the hoop.

To write well, you also need to learn special skills and strategies. We call these skills the **Traits of Good Writing**. You will learn how to build these writing skills in this handbook.

The Traits of Good Writing

Conventions
Correct punctuation, grammar, and spelling

Word Choice
Clear, strong words

Organization
Clear order of ideas

Focus/Ideas
Interesting details about one main idea

Effective Sentences
Different kinds of sentences

Voice
Your own words and ideas

Traits Checklist

The more you write, the easier writing will become for you. As you write, ask yourself these questions.

☑ **FOCUS/IDEAS**	Are my ideas interesting? Do they all tell about my main topic?
☑ **ORGANIZATION**	Are my ideas in a clear order? Do I group ideas in paragraphs?
☑ **VOICE**	Do I use my own words? Do I show how I see things?
☑ **EFFECTIVE SENTENCES**	Are my sentences complete? Do I use both long and short sentences?
☑ **WORD CHOICE**	Do I use words that give my reader a clear picture?
☑ **CONVENTIONS**	Are my spelling, grammar, and punctuation correct?

Try This! Choose a piece of writing from your portfolio. Use the Traits Checklist. What did you do well? What can you improve?

Focus/Ideas

There are many ways to find **topics**, or ideas, for writing. One way is to **brainstorm**. When you brainstorm, you make a list of topics. Then you can look at the list and choose the topic you like the best.

Read these sentences that a student wrote. What is the topic of the sentences?

Student Model

I love to play checkers. My dad often plays with me. Sometimes I win!

The first sentence tells the main idea.

Try This! Find a picture in a book or magazine. Write some words that tell about the picture.

How to Focus Your Writing

What to Do	How to Do It
Brainstorm ideas.	Make a list of topics. Pick topics that are important to you.
Add details.	Ask yourself questions like these: • How does it look? • What does it do? • How do I feel about it?

Try This! Brainstorm a list of animals. Draw one animal from the list. Add interesting details.

Reading ↔ Writing Connection

When you read, you might get ideas for writing. List the ideas in your journal.

Focus/Ideas

Now it's your turn to write.

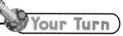

Your Turn

Write a story for your classmates. Tell about something good that happened to you.

Prewrite and Draft

STEP 1 Think of ideas.
Make a list of good things that have happened to you.

STEP 2 Choose an idea.
Who will read the story? Choose an idea that your readers will like.

What is this story about? What happened?

STEP 3 Complete a plan.
Make a flowchart. Show the order of the events.

What happened next?

STEP 4 Write a draft.
Use your flowchart to write sentences.

What happened at the end?

Revise

Share your draft with a few classmates. Talk about how you can make your story better. Use this checklist.

- ☑ My story has a main idea.
- ☑ I have told what happened in order.
- ☑ I have added details.
- ☑ Each sentence tells a complete idea.

Proofread

- ☑ Each sentence begins with a capital letter.
- ☑ Each sentence has an end mark.
- ☑ I have checked my spelling.

Publish and Share

Make a clean copy of your story. Add some pictures of yourself. Show your story to others.

Editor's Marks

∧ Add.

⌃ Change.

𝒆 Take out.

≡ Use a capital letter.

⊙ Add a period.

◯ Check the spelling.

Organization

What is wrong with these directions?

STEP 1 Unlock the door.

STEP 2 Go into the house.

STEP 3 Open the door.

Steps 2 and 3 are out of order.

When you write to explain how to do something, you have to **organize** your facts, or put them in order. If you don't, your readers won't understand what you have to say.

Read these directions. Think about how the writer put the steps in order.

Student Model

What to Do When the Bell Rings

1. Line up by the front door. Stand in ABC order by last name.
2. Walk single file into the room.
3. Sit in your assigned seat.

The title tells what the directions are about.

Each step is included.

The writer uses numbers to put the steps in order.

Try This! Tell classmates how to find an object in the room. See if they can follow your directions.

How to Organize Information

What to Do	How to Do It
Show a clear order.	Put steps in time order.
Use time-order words or numbers.	Use words such as **first, next,** and **last** or numbers such as **1, 2,** and **3.**
Give details to explain the steps.	Use details, such as **Walk single file,** so that readers can picture what to do.

Try This! Find directions for making something. What words does the writer use to put the steps in order?

Writing Forms
Directions give the steps in an activity. They use time-order words and clear details.

For more about how-to writing, see pages 72–73.

Organization

Now you will write a how-to paragraph.

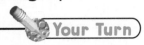

Your Turn

Think of something you can do or something you can make. Write a paragraph telling your classmates how to do or make it.

Prewrite

Make a flowchart like this one to plan your paragraph.

What you need: → Step 1 → Step 2 → Step 3

Draft

STEP 1 **State your topic.**
Tell readers what they are going to learn.

STEP 2 **Tell what things are needed.**
Write a sentence telling all the materials needed.

STEP 3 **Explain the steps in order.**
Follow the plan in your flowchart. Use time-order words. Give details.

Revise

Share your draft with a classmate. Are the steps clear? Use the checklist to help you revise your work.

- ☑ My paragraph names the topic.
- ☑ My paragraph lists the things that are needed.
- ☑ My steps are in the correct order.
- ☑ My directions use clear details.

Proofread

Use this checklist and the Editor's Marks as you proofread your paragraph.

- ☑ I used the correct end marks.
- ☑ I used capital letters correctly.
- ☑ I checked my spelling.

Publish and Share

Make all your revising and proofreading changes. Put a clean copy of your paragraph into a class book.

Voice

Your **writing voice** is the way you say something on paper. Your **personal voice** makes your writing interesting. It helps your readers picture what you are telling and how you feel about your topic.

Read this thank-you note. Find the words and details that show how the writer feels.

Student Model

121 Armadillo Lane
Austin, TX 78753

July 5, 2001

Dear Ben,

Thank you for inviting me to your Fourth of July cookout. I had a great time playing Freeze Tag. I still have the American flag you gave me. It reminds me of the great fun we had.

Your friend,
Tanya

Some details help make word pictures.

Some details show the writer's feelings.

How to Build Your Writing Voice

What to Do	Examples
Add details that help make word pictures.	At the circus, we saw **silly clowns with their faces painted all different colors.**
Add details that show your feelings. Be honest. Be yourself.	I am **lucky** to have so many good friends.

Try This!

Find a picture of a favorite animal in a magazine or a book. Describe the animal, using as many details as you can. Then see if your classmates can guess what animal you chose.

Writing Forms

A friendly letter uses details that help make good word pictures and tell how the writer feels.

For more about writing letters, see pages 54–55.

Voice

Now you will write a friendly letter.

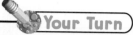

Your Turn

Write a friendly letter to a family member or a friend. Tell about your week.

Prewrite

Make a web to plan what you will write in your letter. In each outside circle, name one thing that happened in the past week.

What Good Writers Do

- Think about your reader.
- Plan what you will write.
- Use words that show how you feel.

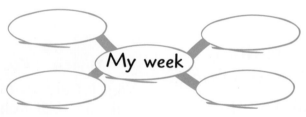

My week

Draft

STEP 1 **Choose a person to whom you will write.**
Write the heading and greeting of your letter.

STEP 2 **Begin in an interesting way.**
Begin as if you are talking to the person. Use the word *you*.

STEP 3 **Use information from your web.**
Follow your plan for the body of your letter. Put events in order. Then, write the closing and your signature.

Revise

Use this checklist to help you revise your writing:

- ☑ My letter follows my plan. I give details and I show how I feel.

- ☑ I show that I care about my reader.

- ☑ My letter has a heading, a greeting, a body, a closing, and a signature.

Proofread

Use this checklist and the Editor's Marks as you proofread your letter.

- ☑ I began each sentence with a capital letter and ended it with the correct punctuation.

- ☑ I checked for capital letters and commas in the heading, greeting, and closing.

- ☑ I checked my spelling.

Editor's Marks

∧ Add.

⌅ Change.

ℯ Take out.

≡ Use a capital letter.

⊙ Add a period.

◯ Check the spelling.

Publish and Share

Write your letter neatly on a clean sheet of paper. Remember to make all of your revising and proofreading changes. In your Writer's Journal, make a list of other people to whom you could write letters.

Word Choice

Imagine that your pet got lost. Friends want to help look for it, but they need to know what to look for. The more clearly you describe your pet, the better your chances of getting it back.

When you write to describe something, you need to choose your words carefully. You want to use the right words to make a clear picture for your reader.

Read this student's poem. Think about how the words paint a picture.

Student Model

Fuzzy Bunny

I have a little fuzzy bunny.

He thinks that carrots taste so yummy.

He's white and has a small black spot.

It looks just like a polka-dot.

He loves to twitch his wet pink nose.

All day long it goes and goes.

Sometimes I rub his silky tummy.

Isn't my little bunny funny?

What does the spot look like?

Colorful words show how the bunny looks.

The writer tells how the bunny feels.

Strategies for Choosing Words

What to Do	Examples
Use interesting verbs to describe actions.	The bunny loves to **twitch** his nose.
Use nouns that name one thing instead of a whole group of things.	The bunny thinks **carrots** taste yummy.
Compare one thing to another to make a word picture.	The small **black spot** looks just like a **polka-dot**.
Use words that tell how things look, feel, smell, sound, and taste.	**fuzzy** bunny, **silky** tummy

Try This! Find a poem and a story. Which one has more details about how things look, feel, sound, smell, or taste? Give examples of the colorful words each writer uses.

Writing Forms

A good description uses colorful words and details.

For more about writing that describes, see pages 60–61.

Word Choice

Now you will write a paragraph that describes.

 **Your Turn**

Choose an animal. Write a paragraph to describe that animal to a classmate.

- Think of what will interest your readers.
- Describe your topic so that your readers can picture it.

Prewrite

Make a web to plan your paragraph.

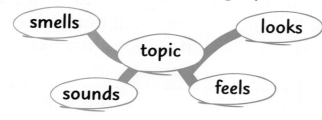

smells

looks

topic

sounds

feels

Draft

Follow these steps to help you write.

STEP 1 **Write a topic sentence.**
Tell your topic and your main idea.

STEP 2 **Use ideas from your web.**
Use your web to write sentences that describe.

STEP 3 **Use colorful words.**
Make a word picture for your reader.

Revise

Share your description with a partner. Use this checklist to make changes.

☑ I make clear word pictures.

☑ I use colorful words to add details.

☑ I use words that tell how the animal looks, feels, sounds, or smells.

☑ My paragraph has a topic sentence and detail sentences.

Proofread

Use this checklist as you proofread.

☑ I ended each sentence with the correct punctuation mark.

☑ I used capital letters where needed.

☑ I checked my spelling.

☑ I left margins on both sides of the paper.

Editor's Marks

∧ Add.

⌃ Change.

℘ Take out.

≡ Use a capital letter.

⊙ Add a period.

◯ Check the spelling.

Publish and Share

Make a neat copy of your paragraph, and share it with classmates. Tell what you like best about your classmates' descriptions.

Effective Sentences

Good sentences tell complete thoughts. They put words in a clear order.

Good sentences also work together. One sentence leads smoothly to another. Writers mix short sentences and long sentences. They use statements and questions and exclamations.

Read this paragraph. Think about how the writer used different kinds of sentences.

Student Model

Horses and zebras are alike in many ways. They are both hoofed mammals, and they can run fast. Both have long tails. Both have a mane. Horses and zebras both like to eat grass, too. Still, it is easy to tell these two animals apart. No horse has black and white stripes like a zebra!

The writer starts with the main idea.

The writer uses a mix of long and short sentences.

The exclamation adds interest.

Try This! Read a nonfiction article in a magazine. Does the writer use different kinds of sentences? Give some examples.

How to Write Effective Sentences

What to Do	How to Do It
Write clear sentences.	Check to see if each sentence has a naming part and a telling part.
Combine sentences.	Put sentences together. **Example:** They are both hoofed mammals, **and** they can run fast.
Use different kinds of sentences.	Use some long sentences and some short ones. Include statements, questions, and exclamations.

Try This! Choose one paragraph about a science topic from a book. Think about how you could give the same information using different types of sentences.

Effective Sentences

Write a paragraph that uses different kinds of sentences.

Your Turn

Choose your favorite day of the week at school. Write a paragraph for a family member, telling what you do on that day.

What Good Writers Do

- Think about what your reader would want to know.
- Include facts and your own thoughts.

Prewrite

List the most important things you do on that day. Add one detail about each item.

1. ___   Detail: ___
2. ___   Detail: ___
3. ___   Detail: ___

Draft

Follow these steps as you write.

STEP 1 **State your topic.**
Tell what you are writing about.

STEP 2 **Organize your ideas.**
Put the events in order. Add details.

STEP 3 **Write an ending sentence.**
Tell what you like most about the day.

Revise

Use these questions to help you revise your paragraph.

☑ Do you use different kinds of sentences?

☑ Is your information well organized?

☑ Can you add details to tell more about your topic?

Proofread

Use this checklist and the Editor's Marks as you proofread your paragraph.

☑ Each sentence tells a complete thought.

☑ Each sentence begins with a capital letter and ends with an end mark.

☑ You have checked your spelling.

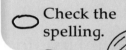

Editor's Marks

∧ Add.

⌃ Change.

ℒ Take out.

≡ Use a capital letter.

⊙ Add a period.

◯ Check the spelling.

Publish and Share

Make a neat copy of your paragraph. Read it aloud to a small group of classmates, or take it home to share with family members.

Conventions

You must follow some rules when you write. These rules are called **conventions**. You proofread to make sure you are following the rules. Here are some ideas to use as you proofread.

Proofreading Strategies

Wait before proofreading. Put your writing away. Then look at it again later.

Proofread in steps.

1. First, look at **sentences**. Do they make sense?

2. Then check **capital letters** and **end marks**.

3. Last, check your **spelling**.

Read your writing out loud. You may hear where you need a comma, a period, or a question mark.

 Technology

A computer can help you
- add or take out words easily.
- check your spelling.
- find a better word.

Proofreading Checklist

These questions will help you proofread your work.

Grammar

- ☑ Does every sentence have a naming part and a telling part?
- ☑ Does each sentence begin with a capital letter?
- ☑ Does each verb have the correct ending?

Spelling

- ☑ Are you sure of the spelling of every word?
- ☑ Have you spelled plural nouns correctly?

 Technology

Did you type your work on a computer? Use the spell checker to help you spell words correctly. Then check the spelling again yourself.

Sharing Your Work

There are many ways to share your writing. The way you choose depends on the type of writing it is.

Here are some ideas for publishing your writing. You can probably think of other ideas, too.

Sharing Any Kind of Writing
- Read it aloud.
- Have a partner read it silently.
- Pin it to a bulletin board.
- Send it in an e-mail.

Sharing Descriptions
- Draw pictures that go with your description.
- Read your work aloud. Play soft music in the background.
- Make up a dance to go with your writing.

Sharing Stories

- Work with a partner or in a group. Act out your story.
- Draw pictures to go with your story.
- Read your story aloud to another class.
- Make a class storybook.
- Send your story to a children's magazine.

What Good Writers Do

- Leave margins.
- Write neatly.
- Indent each paragraph.
- Put your name on your work.

Uppercase
Manuscript Alphabet

A B C D E F G

H I J K L M N

O P Q R S T

U V W X Y Z

A B C D E F G

H I J K L M N

O P Q R S T

U V W X Y Z

Lowercase
Manuscript Alphabet

Uppercase
Cursive Alphabet

A B C D E F G

H I J K L M N

O P Q R S T

U V W X Y Z

A B C D E F G

H I J K L M N

O P Q R S T

U V W X Y Z

Lowercase Cursive Alphabet

a b c d e f g

h i j k l m n

o p q r s t

u v w x y z

a b c d e f g

h i j k l m n

o p q r s t

u v w x y z

D'Nealian
Manuscript Alphabet

ABCDEFG
HIJKLMN
OPQRST
UVWXYZ

abcdefg
hijklmn
opqrst
uvwxyz

D'Nealian
Cursive Alphabet

A B C D E F G H
I J K L M N O P
Q R S T U V W
X Y Z

a b c d e f g h
i j k l m n o
p q r s t u v
w x y z

Elements of Handwriting

Shape

Do not put loops in these letters or leave spaces.
Make retrace strokes smooth.

correct

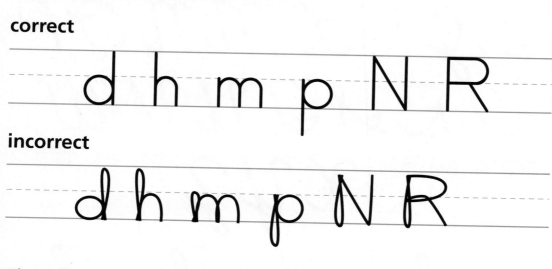

incorrect

Close circle letters. Connect lines.

correct

incorrect

Elements of Handwriting

Spacing Letters

Letters should not be written too close together or too far apart.

just right   **too close**   **too far apart**

play   play   p l a y

Spacing Words

The space between words should be as wide as a pencil.

United States

Spacing Sentences

Leave a pencil space between sentences.

He sang. He danced.

Elements of Handwriting

Position

Write all letters so they sit on the bottom line.

correct   incorrect

John   John

Size

Write tall letters to touch the top line.
Write tail letters to go below the bottom line.
Write short letters to touch the midline.

correct   incorrect

Monday   Monday

Stroke

Make your letters smooth and even.
They should not be too light or too dark.

smooth and even   **too light**   **too dark**

mop   mop   mop

Common Errors

incorrect   **correct**

Curve the tail stroke on **q** to the right.
The **q** could look like **g**.

incorrect   **correct**

Start at the midline.
The **y** could look like uppercase **Y**.

incorrect   **correct**

Do not loop **i**.
The **i** could look like **e**.

incorrect   **correct**

Touch the top line.
The **l** could look like **e**.

incorrect   **correct**

Be sure the slant stroke returns to the bottom line.
The **u** could look like **v**.

Peer Conferences

Sometimes, you will get together with classmates to share your writing. This is a **peer conference**. Hearing what your classmates have to say about your work can help you make it better.

Here are some ideas to use during a peer conference.

Strategies for Speakers

What to Do	How to Do It
Read your work aloud.	• Read slowly and clearly. • When you finish reading, ask whether your ideas were clear.
Talk about the work of others.	• Tell exactly what you like, and why. Tell what doesn't work, and why. • Be polite. Give ideas for making the work better.

Strategies for Listeners

What to Do	How to Do It
Be an active listener.	• Watch the speaker. Don't talk or move. • Listen for the main idea and the details.
Take notes.	• Write down ideas about your classmate's writing. • Write down what classmates say about your writing.
Keep an open mind.	• Use your classmates' ideas to make your own work better.

Using Rubrics

Your teacher may use a rubric to grade your writing. A **rubric** is like a checklist. The best writing has each of the key traits on the checklist.

Here is how to use a rubric.

Before Writing

- Read the rubric to find out what your writing should include.
- Think about the key traits as you begin planning to write.

During Writing

- Check your draft against the rubric.
- Put a mark next to each trait that is missing.
- Use the marked rubric as you revise your draft.

After Writing

- Make sure your writing shows all the key traits on the rubric.
- You may need to revise your draft again. Make a clean copy.

What Good Writers Do

- Be sure you do everything you are asked to do.
- Write neatly.
- Spell correctly. Check your dictionary if you're unsure of a word.

Writing for Tests

A writing test gives you a topic to write about. The topic and the directions for writing are stated in a writing **prompt**. Here is an example.

Your Turn

Think about your favorite season. ← what to write
Write a paragraph about that season.
Explain why it is your favorite. ← purpose

topic →

Here is what one student wrote.

Student Model

My favorite season is summer. I like summer because I go on vacation. We drive to Florida to visit my grandparents. We go to the beach, and we go on a boat in the lake. Once I saw an alligator! I also like summer because I don't have homework. I can just read and play outside. I am sad when summer ends.

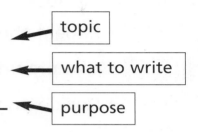

How to Take a Writing Test

STEP 1 **Read the prompt carefully.**

- Find the topic, purpose, and type of writing.
- Repeat the assignment to yourself.

STEP 2 **Make prewriting notes.**

- Decide on your focus.
- List or draw your ideas.
- Put ideas in an order that makes sense.

STEP 3 **Use your notes to write a draft.**

- Write a sentence that tells your topic.
- Add details.
- Write neatly.

STEP 4 **Proofread your writing.**

- Make sure your sentences are complete.
- Make sure each sentence starts with a capital letter and ends with an end mark.

Writing Models

Sentences About a Picture

A **sentence** tells a complete thought. It begins with a capital letter. It ends with an end mark.

- Choose an idea.

- Draw a picture that shows your idea.

- Write a sentence that tells the main idea of your picture.

- Be sure your sentence has a naming part and a telling part.

My dad likes to paint trees and the sky.

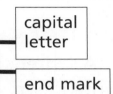

capital letter

end mark

Writer's Journal

A **writer's journal** is a place where you can write down your thoughts or important ideas. Writing in your journal helps you keep a record of interesting things that happen.

- **Write the date.**
- **Write about interesting things that happened.**
- **Tell why these things are important to you.**

September 2, 200—

Today was my first piano lesson. I was so nervous. But I loved playing! The half hour flew by. My teacher said I did a great job!

date

what happened

how the writer feels

Paragraph

A **paragraph** is a group of sentences that tell about one main idea. A paragraph begins with a topic sentence. The **topic sentence** tells the main idea. The other sentences are called detail sentences. **Detail sentences** tell about the main idea.

- Write a topic sentence that tells the main idea of your paragraph.

- Indent the first line.

- Write detail sentences that tell about the main idea.

I like going to the fair. The roller coaster is my favorite ride. I was scared the first time I rode it. Now I think it is a lot of fun. I also like playing the games and winning prizes.

topic sentence

detail sentences

Personal Story

In a **personal story**, a writer tells about something that has happened in his or her life. A personal story can tell how the writer feels about something. It uses words like *I, me,* and *my.*

- Think of things that have happened in your life. Choose one to tell about.

- Write your story in the order in which things happened. Use time-order words like <u>first</u>, <u>next</u>, <u>then</u>, and <u>last</u>.

- Use words like <u>I</u> and <u>me</u> to tell about yourself.

Personal Story

It was the last inning. We were behind by one run. There were two outs, and then I was at bat.

I swung at the first pitch and missed. Strike one! Then I hit a foul ball. Strike two! On the next pitch, I kept my eye on the ball. I hit the ball hard and started to run. At first, I didn't hear the cheers. Then I knew. Finally, I had hit my first home run!

Time-order words help show the order in which things happen.

Using both long and short sentences adds interest.

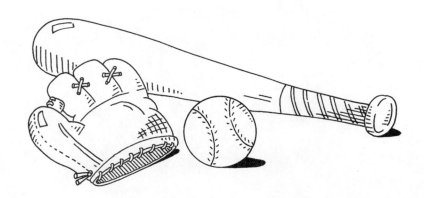

Story

A **story** tells about real or make-believe events. A story has a beginning, a middle, and an ending.

• Write a beginning. Tell who the characters are, where the story takes place, and what the problem is.

• Write the middle. Tell what happens to the characters. Tell what they do.

• Write the ending. Tell how the problem is solved.

• Write a title for your story.

Junior Vet

I think I might want to be a veterinarian someday. So I asked Dr. Curry if I could help her out for a week. Dr. Curry let me feed the animals and watch her work. At the end of the week, she asked if I still wanted to be an animal doctor. "More than ever," I answered. I meant every word!

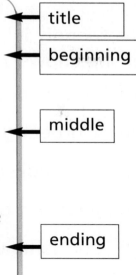

title

beginning

middle

ending

Friendly Letter

In a **friendly letter**, a writer writes to someone he or she knows. A friendly letter has five parts.

• Write your address and the date as the heading.

• Write a greeting to say hello.

• Write a friendly message in the body.

• Write a closing to end your letter.

• Sign your name under the closing.

Friendly Letter

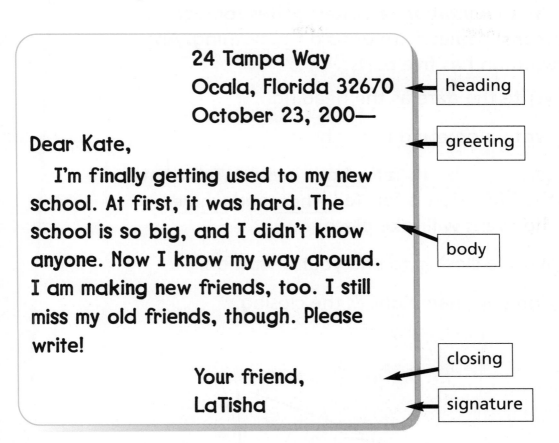

24 Tampa Way
Ocala, Florida 32670 ← heading
October 23, 200—

Dear Kate, ← greeting

    I'm finally getting used to my new
school. At first, it was hard. The
school is so big, and I didn't know
anyone. Now I know my way around. ← body
I am making new friends, too. I still
miss my old friends, though. Please
write!

          Your friend, ← closing
          LaTisha ← signature

Invitation

In an **invitation**, a writer invites someone to come somewhere or to do something. An invitation has five parts.

• Write the date as the heading.

• Write a greeting to say hello.

• Write the body. Tell <u>who</u> is invited. Tell <u>what</u> the invitation is for. Tell <u>when</u> and <u>where</u> the event will take place.

• Write a closing to end your invitation.

• Sign your name under the closing.

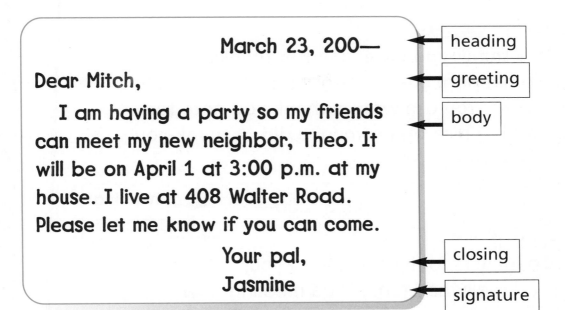

March 23, 200— ← heading

Dear Mitch, ← greeting

I am having a party so my friends ← body
can meet my new neighbor, Theo. It
will be on April 1 at 3:00 p.m. at my
house. I live at 408 Walter Road.
Please let me know if you can come.

Your pal, ← closing
Jasmine ← signature

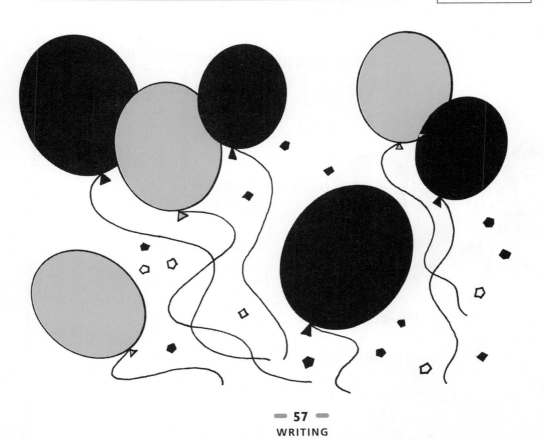

Thank-You Note

In a **thank-you note**, a writer thanks someone for something. You can write a thank-you note for a gift. You can write a thank-you note for something nice that someone did. A thank-you note has five parts.

April 3, 200— ← heading

Dear Jasmine, ← greeting

Thank you for inviting me to your party. I really had fun. I liked meeting Theo, too. Maybe he will join our team this summer. ← body

Your friend, ← closing

Mitch ← signature

Envelope

An **envelope** is used to send a letter.

The **return address** names the person who is sending the letter.

The **mailing address** names the person who will get the letter.

Kayla Wicker
162 Magnolia Street
Pomona, California 93944

return address

Sharon Johnson
2909 Buck Run Drive
Richmond, Virginia 23261

mailing address

Paragraph That Describes

In a **paragraph that describes**, a writer describes a person, an animal, a place, or a thing. The writer uses describing words that tell what people see, hear, taste, smell, and feel.

- Write a topic sentence to tell who or what your paragraph is about.

- Write sentences that tell what the person, animal, place, or thing is like.

- Use words that give a good word picture.

My family went to visit Mammoth Cave in Kentucky. It is a very big cave. It is cold and dark on the inside. When the flashlights are turned off, you can't even see your hands! The walls are wet and feel slimy. The whole cave has a damp smell.

topic sentence

describing words in detail sentences

The writer uses words that tell how things look, feel and smell.

Poem

In a **poem**, a writer describes something in an interesting way. Poems often have a **rhythm**, or **beat**, that makes them fun to read. Some poems have rhyming words.

Other poems do not rhyme. All kinds of poems "paint" word pictures with colorful words.

- Paint a good word picture.

- Use rhyming words if you want to.

- Give your poem a title.

New Neighbor

The moving van is here.
And what is that I see?
A bike that's just like mine
And one new friend for me!

title

rhyme

Night Sounds

The train rumbles and horns honk.
Footsteps pass my window.
Voices shout hello.
These are the night sounds in my
    neighborhood.

title

no rhyme

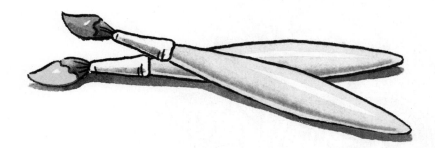

Paragraph That Gives Information

In a **paragraph that gives information**, a writer gives facts and details about one topic.

- Write a topic sentence. Tell who or what your paragraph is about.

- Indent the first line.

- Write detail sentences. Give interesting facts about the person, animal, place, or thing.

Many African American people celebrate Kwanzaa. It is a celebration of the customs and history of African American people. It is a gathering time for families, like Thanksgiving.

The holiday is celebrated for seven days. It begins the day after Christmas. On each night of Kwanzaa, a candle is lit. Each candle stands for a rule to help people live their lives.

topic sentence

detail sentences

A new main idea needs a new paragraph.

Paragraph That Explains

In a **paragraph that explains,** a writer tells how something happens or why it happens.

- Indent the first line of the paragraph.

- Write a topic sentence. Tell what you are going to explain.

- Write detail sentences. Include important facts that help explain your topic.

- Put the details in an order that makes sense.

- Write a title that tells what your paragraph is about.

Paragraph That Explains

title

How Seeds Grow into Plants

Many full-size plants grow from little seeds. For example, sunflowers, carrots, and even tall pine trees all come from tiny seeds. Most seeds have an outer covering called a seed coat. Inside are a tiny plant and some stored food. The small plant uses the stored food to grow. Soon the little plant breaks through the seed coat. It grows its own roots, stems, and leaves. In time, the seed grows into a full-size plant.

topic sentence

facts

Book Report

A **book report** tells what a book is about. It names the title, the author, and the illustrator of the book. It also tells what someone thinks about the book.

- Write the title of the book.

- Write the author's name. Write the illustrator's name, if there is one.

- Write sentences that tell what the book is about. Tell about important people, places, and things.

- Write what you think about the book. Tell why you like or do not like the book.

<u>**The Popcorn Dragon**</u> ← title

by Jane Thayer ← author

pictures by Lisa McCue ← illustrator

A dragon named Dexter liked to blow smoke. He wanted to have friends. The other animals didn't like him because he was always showing off. Then Dexter discovered he could use his hot breath to make something special. ← what the book is about

Play

In a **play**, an author writes a story to act out. People play the parts of the characters in the story.

• Think of a story to tell.

• Decide what characters are in the story.

• Decide when and where the story takes place.

• Write what the characters say.

• Write what the characters do.

CHARACTERS: MOTHER, GWEN, BANTA (a rabbit)

characters

TIME: morning

when

SETTING: a garden

where

MOTHER: Gwen, I'm going to the office. While I'm gone, please plant the garden.

what characters say

GWEN: Yes, Mother. (Mother leaves.)

what characters do

BANTA: Come play with me!

GWEN: Who said that?

BANTA: I did.

How-to Paragraph

In a **how-to paragraph**, a writer gives directions that tell how to make or do something. The steps are in order.

• Write a sentence to name your topic.

• Write a sentence that tells what things are needed.

• Write steps in the correct order to tell how to make or do something.

• Use the words <u>first</u>, <u>next</u>, <u>then</u>, and <u>last</u> to show the order of the steps.

Did you know that you can water your plants even when you're not home? You'll need thin cotton rope and a glass of water. First, put the glass of water next to your plant. Next, push one end of the rope into the soil. Last, put the other end of the rope in the water. The water will travel through the rope from the glass to the plant.

topic sentence

things that are needed

steps

Time-order words tell when to do each step.

Research Report

To write a **research report**, a writer gathers information from different books and magazines and takes **notes**. Then he or she uses the notes to write about the topic.

• Take notes about your topic.

• Use your notes to write a few paragraphs about your topic.

• Give your research report a title.

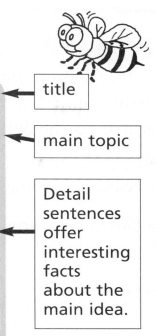

Busy as a Bee

title

There are three kinds of honeybees. The queen bee is the biggest. Her job is to lay eggs in the nest. Male bees are the drones. It is their job to help the queen. The smallest bees are the worker bees. Worker bees collect nectar from flowers and bring it back to the nest. Other worker bees make honey from the nectar.

main topic

Detail sentences offer interesting facts about the main idea.

Poster That Persuades

In a **poster that persuades**, a writer shows a problem. He or she draws a picture and writes words to show how the problem could be solved.

• Decide on a topic. What is the problem? How could it be solved?

• Write your ideas about the picture.

Grammar, Usage, and Mechanics

SENTENCES

- A **sentence** tells a complete thought.
- It begins with a capital letter.
- It ends with an end mark.
- The words are in an order that makes sense.

Tell whether each group of words is a sentence.

1. **We go to the library.**

2. **lots of books.**

3. **The room is quiet.**

4. **Not talking or yelling.**

Write each group of words as a correct sentence.

5. **i read a good book**

6. **story this funny is**

7. **lucy reads aloud**

8. **children the are quiet**

SENTENCES

Write this report on "Lucy's Quiet Book" correctly. Begin each sentence with a capital letter, and end each sentence with an end mark. Make sure the words are in an order that makes sense.

	Lucy's Quiet Book
	a girl had six brothers. Too much noise they made. she read aloud to them. then they were quiet. Very much I liked this story

CUMULATIVE REVIEW

Tell which groups of words are sentences and which are not.

1. **The library in town.**
2. **Reading a good book.**
3. **That one was funny.**
4. **You can read it to me.**
5. **When I listen to a story.**

Write each group of words as a correct sentence.

6. **a man wrote this book**
7. **The librarian it read.**
8. **the children laughed**
9. **The story funny was.**
10. **What part you like did?**

STATEMENTS AND QUESTIONS

Skill Reminder

- A **statement** is a sentence that tells something. It ends with a period (.).

- A **question** is a sentence that asks something. It ends with a question mark (?).

Tell whether each group of words is a statement or a question.

1. **Where is Mudge?**

2. **He is outside.**

3. **Who is his friend?**

4. **Henry is his friend.**

Write each sentence. Add the correct end mark.

5. **The leaves are falling**

6. **Is the wind cold**

7. **Can we play outside**

8. **We rake the leaves**

STATEMENTS AND QUESTIONS

Henry talked with his dad about his walk with his dog, Mudge. His dad asked questions. Henry answered. Write each group of words. Add end marks to make each group of words a question or a statement.

1. Where did you go

2. We took a walk

3. Did you have fun

4. It was lots of fun

5. What did you see

6. Birds were flying south

CUMULATIVE REVIEW

Write each group of words as a correct sentence.

1. Henry for a walk went.
2. He his dog took along.
3. They some chipmunks saw.
4. The leaves falling were.
5. some leaves were red
6. did they eat apples
7. what did Mudge do
8. he chased a chipmunk
9. Henry threw to him the ball.
10. Mudge can run fast

COMMANDS AND EXCLAMATIONS

- A **command** is a sentence that tells someone to do something. It ends with a period (.).
- An **exclamation** is a sentence that shows strong feeling. It ends with an exclamation point (!).

Tell whether each sentence is a command or an exclamation.

1. **What a nice friend you are!**
2. **Please give me a basket.**
3. **Follow me to the island.**
4. **How warm it is here!**

Write each sentence. Add the correct end mark.

5. **Hand me a sandwich**
6. **This tastes so good**
7. **What fine tea you made**
8. **Please wipe your mouth**

COMMANDS AND EXCLAMATIONS

Frog and Toad are talking. Write each group of words. Add end marks to make each group of words a command or an exclamation.

1. What a nice day it is
2. Come fishing with me
3. What a good idea that is
4. Oh no, I can't go
5. Give me your pole
6. Catch a fish for me

Copy the chart. Write Frog and Toad's sentences in the chart where they belong.

COMMANDS	EXCLAMATIONS

CUMULATIVE REVIEW

Write each sentence. Add the correct end mark.

1. Watch that green frog
2. What a long tongue it has
3. What is it looking for
4. Many frogs eat bugs
5. Is it quicker than a fly
6. Listen to the noise it makes
7. How loud it is
8. I took a picture of it
9. Does the frog like the rain
10. Of course it does

NAMING PARTS OF SENTENCES

Skill Reminder

- A sentence has a **naming part**. It names who or what the sentence is about.
- Naming parts can name two people or things. The word *and* is used to join them.

Write each sentence. Draw a line under the naming part.

1. **Our school is very big.**

2. **Many children go there.**

3. **That boy is in my class.**

4. **He always sits by himself.**

5. **His desk and chair are in the corner.**

Complete the sentences by writing a naming part.

6. ___ **liked that game.**

7. ___ **played it well.**

8. ___ **stayed inside.**

9. ___ **and** ___ **walked to school.**

10. ___ **and** ___ **were in my bookbag.**

NAMING PARTS OF SENTENCES

Read Wilson's note to Sara. Tell what the naming part is for each sentence.

Dear Sara,

(1) School was hard for me.

(2) The other kids left me alone. (3) I felt sad.

(4) I like to play with the other kids now.

(5) You helped me a lot.

Your friend,

Wilson

Sara is writing about her first week at school. Complete the sentences by writing a naming part.

6. ___ went to a new school.

7. ___ were nice to me.

8. ___ played outside.

9. ___ read some stories.

10. ___ and ___ built a snowman.

CUMULATIVE REVIEW

Read the sentences. Choose the best way to write each underlined section.

(1) <u>Think about being new at school?</u> It can be scary.
(2) <u>Sara her brother</u> are new. Sara is in Wilson's class.
(3) <u>Wilson sits alone.</u> Sara plays with Wilson.
(4) <u>What a kind person she is.</u>

1. **Think about. Being new at school.**
   Think about being new at school.
   Think about being new at school
   No mistake

2. **Sara. her brother.**
   Her brother Sara
   Sara and her brother
   No mistake

3. **Wilson sits alone?**
   Wilson sits alone
   Wilson? Sits alone.
   No mistake

4. **What kind of person she is?**
   What a kind person she is?
   What a kind person she is!
   No mistake

TELLING PARTS OF SENTENCES

Write each sentence. Draw two lines under the telling part of each sentence.

1. **This zoo is lots of fun.**
2. **I like the snakes best.**
3. **The chameleons catch flies.**
4. **Their colors are beautiful.**
5. **One tiny chameleon hides.**

Complete the sentences by writing a telling part.

6. **The frogs ___ .**
7. **A zoo worker ___ .**
8. **That large snake ___ .**
9. **The elephant ___ and ___ .**
10. **A big turtle ___ and ___ .**

TELLING PARTS OF SENTENCES

Write each sentence. Draw two lines under the telling part of each sentence.

1. **All people walk on the path.**

2. **Children stay in their groups.**

3. **People keep off the grass.**

4. **Zookeepers feed the animals.**

5. **Cars stay off the path.**

6. **Pets cannot come in.**

7.–10. Match the naming parts with the telling parts. Write a complete sentence for each pair.

NAMING PARTS	TELLING PARTS
Seals	hide in shells.
Elephants	run fast.
Turtles	are strong.
Deer	are funny.

CUMULATIVE REVIEW

Write each sentence. Draw one line under the naming part and two lines under the telling part of each sentence.

1. We went to the zoo on Friday.

2. My sister wanted to see the polar bears.

3. The baby bear jumped up and down.

4. Many small children laughed.

5. A big polar bear was sleeping.

6. I liked him the best.

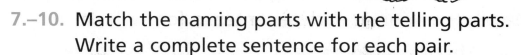

7.–10. Match the naming parts with the telling parts. Write a complete sentence for each pair.

NAMING PARTS	TELLING PARTS
Cats	bark and swim
Bees	run and roar
Seals	buzz and fly
Tigers	nap and purr

NOUNS

Skill Reminder

• A **noun** names a person, place, thing, or animal.

Write the noun from each group of words.

1. **crow, flying, up**
2. **planted, field, dry**
3. **wide, fence, old**
4. **smiled, noisy, tractor**
5. **once, pulled, farmer**

Write the noun in each sentence.

6. **That man works hard.**
7. **Look at his hands.**
8. **The shovel is heavy.**
9. **Where is the horse?**
10. **Ride in the wagon.**
11. **His wife is waiting.**
12. **A sandwich would taste good.**

NOUNS

Look at the picture. Copy the chart. Then write two nouns for each type of noun found in the shaded boxes.

PERSON	ANIMAL	PLACE	THING

CUMULATIVE REVIEW

Write each sentence. Draw one line under the naming part and two lines under the telling part of each sentence.

1. **The farmer has a hard job.**
2. **Turnips grow in his garden.**
3. **One small rabbit eats many plants.**
4. **A scarecrow scares the birds.**
5. **That dog chases other animals.**
6. **The crops need lots of water.**
7. **Sunlight helps the plants to grow.**
8. **The farmer picks the vegetables.**
9.–16. Read the sentences above and write two nouns from each.

PLURAL NOUNS

- Add the letter *s* to most nouns to name more than one.
- Add the letters *es* to some nouns to name more than one.

Write each sentence. Circle the nouns in each sentence that name more than one.

1. **The girls plant some bushes.**
2. **Drop seeds into these holes.**
3. **Our classes paid for those trees.**
4. **The benches have wide seats.**
5. **Some flowers grow in pots.**

Write each noun, making it name more than one.

6. **box**
7. **rose**
8. **pail**
9. **lunch**
10. **vase**
11. **dress**
12. **hose**
13. **bird**
14. **rash**
15. **fence**

PLURAL NOUNS

Read the story. Make the nouns that follow the numbers name more than one.

Mom needed help cleaning her office. First, I put away three **(1)** letter. Then, I packed four **(2)** box. I put nine **(3)** pen away. I cleaned some **(4)** dish. I put all her **(5)** clip into two **(6)** drawer. After that, I hung up her two **(7)** phone and dusted all the **(8)** picture. You could see some **(9)** patch of her desk! When Mom saw this, she gave me ten **(10)** kiss.

CUMULATIVE REVIEW

Write each sentence. Circle the nouns.

1. The class did an important job.
2. Each student helped with the trail.
3. One group drew a map.
4. One girl carried a box.
5. The teacher looked at her book.

6.–10. Make each noun in the sentences above name more than one.

MORE PLURAL NOUNS

Skill Reminder

• Some nouns change their spelling to name more than one.

Make each noun name more than one.

1. **woman**
2. **foot**
3. **goose**
4. **child**
5. **tooth**
6. **mouse**

Write each sentence. Use the correct noun.

7. **Two (man, men) flew the plane.**
8. **The plane flew over a (goose, geese).**
9. **A small (child, children) laughed.**
10. **The plane landed ten (foot, feet) away.**

MORE PLURAL NOUNS

1.–5. Read the story. Write the five nouns that name more than one.

> I visited the toy store. Three tin men stood on a shelf. I liked the four dancing women. A stuffed alligator had many teeth. Many children were in the store. They stamped their feet when it was time to go.

6.–10. Make each noun you wrote name only one.

CUMULATIVE REVIEW

Make each noun name more than one.

1. wing
2. bush
3. man
4. pilot
5. child
6. bench

Write each sentence. Use the correct noun.

7. A (mouse/mice) saw a plane.
8. It went behind those (tree/trees).
9. Two (fox/foxes) came to look.
10. They showed their (tooth/teeth).
11. Three (deer/deers) helped the mice.
12. All of the (animal/animals) became friends.

NAMES OF PEOPLE

Skill Reminder

- **Proper nouns** begin with capital letters.
- Names of people are proper nouns.
- **Titles** of people begin with capital letters. Most titles are short forms of words. They often end with periods.

Write each name correctly. Add capital letters and periods.

1. gary newton
2. nancy druthers
3. asa darling
4. steve cortese

5. dr lee fields
6. mrs ling
7. mr bob james
8. miss antonia smith

Give these people names and titles.

9.

10.

NAMES OF PEOPLE

Hedgehog is making a list of people to invite to a party. Write each name correctly.

1. dr laura gorman

2. cindy crow

3. mrs lumbly

4. chip mayer

5. mr harvey gold

6. rita starks

7. ray singh

8. miss bertha kats

9. mrs lynn wong

10. dr miguel sanchez

CUMULATIVE REVIEW

Read the sentences. Choose the best way to write each group of underlined words.

Alonzo baked a birthday cake **(1)** for his friend Rosie. He poured flour and milk into a bowl. **(2)** He carefully cracked three egges. **(3)** Mrs Sanchez put the cake in the oven. **(4)** The childs at the party loved the cake.

1. his friend Rosie for.
   for his Friend Rosie.
   for his friend rosie.
   No mistake

2. He carefully cracked. Three egges.
   Three egges he carefully cracked.
   He carefully cracked three eggs.
   No mistake

3. Put the cake in the oven, Mrs Sanchez.
   Mrs. Sanchez put the cake in the oven.
   Mrs sanchez put the cake in the oven.
   No mistake

4. The party childs loved the cake.
   The children at the party loved the cake.
   The childs at the partys loved the cake.
   No mistake

ANIMALS AND PLACES

1.–6. The Kids' Club is having a pet show. Make name tags for the animals. Write each name from the box correctly.

| scruffy   miss todd   hoosier   sam   susie   rex |

7.–10. Read the invitation to the pet show. Write the place names correctly.

110 elm street
newton, ohio

Please come to our pet show. It
will be at 4:00 at 310 west road.
If it rains, we will move to
242 highland drive.

ANIMALS AND PLACES

Skill Reminder

- Names of places begin with capital letters.
- Names of animals begin with capital letters.

Write each city and state name correctly.

1. **orlando, florida**
2. **denver, colorado**
3. **houston, texas**
4. **newark, new jersey**
5. **kansas city, kansas**

Write each sentence correctly.

6. **I found rover on second avenue.**
7. **Could tweety fly all the way to maine?**
8. **I bought fluffy at the store on main street.**

CUMULATIVE REVIEW

Write each proper name correctly.

1. mr jed jenkins
2. dr margaret myles
3. portland, oregon
4. main street
5. sparky
6. fluffy

Write each sentence correctly.

7. sheri has a bird named mr tibbs.
8. They live at 24 lark lane.
9. danny is from muncie, indiana.
10. jan has a hamster named smokey.
11. This summer I will travel to san diego.
12. My school is on orchard street.

NAMES OF DAYS

- The **names of days** are proper nouns.
- The names of days begin with capital letters.

1.–7. Look at the calendar. Write the name of each day correctly.

sunday	monday	tuesday	wednesday	thursday	friday	saturday

Write each sentence correctly.

8. **Last saturday we picked apples.**

9. **Mom made apple crisp on sunday.**

10. **We ate all of it tuesday night.**

1.–5. The children in Ms. Jenkin's class are planning to put on the play "Johnny Appleseed." Their plan is not in order. Write the plan correctly, putting it in order.

	thursday
	Try on costumes.
	friday
	Put on the play.
	monday
	Read the play aloud.
	wednesday
	Choose parts.
	tuesday
	Paint the backdrop.

6.–7. Write two sentences that tell what you like to do on the weekend. Use the name of a day of the week in each sentence.

CUMULATIVE REVIEW

Write each proper noun correctly.

1. mr john chapman
2. wednesday
3. chicago, illinois
4. tuesday
5. apple tree lane

Write each sentence correctly.

6. johnny appleseed walked here.
7. He started in pennsylvania.
8. He walked every day except sunday.
9. mr appleseed's feet must have hurt on saturdays!
10. Did he walk all the way to california?

NAMES OF MONTHS

Write each date correctly.

1. october 5

2. january 12

3. april 29

4. july 4

Write each sentence correctly.

5. Spring lasts from march until june.

6. Summer lasts from june until september.

7. Fall lasts from september until december.

8. Winter lasts from december until march.

NAMES OF MONTHS

1.–12. The months are mixed up. Write them in the correct order.

February

October

April

September

January

March

June

November

May

August

December

July

13.–14. Write two sentences that tell what you like to do during one month of the year.

Example: I like to pick apples in October.

CUMULATIVE REVIEW

Write the days and months correctly.

1. **tuesday, november 6**
2. **friday, june 17**
3. **sunday, february 20**
4. **wednesday, august 22**
5. **monday, march 1**

Write each sentence correctly.

6. **We planted seeds on april 25.**
7. **The plants sprouted on may 12.**
8. **I picked flowers last tuesday.**
9. **I will water the garden on friday.**
10. **New blooms will grow in july.**

NAMES OF HOLIDAYS

Skill Reminder

- Important words in the **names of holidays** begin with capital letters.

Write each holiday correctly.

1. **arbor day**

2. **valentine's day**

3. **independence day**

4. **thanksgiving**

Write each sentence correctly.

5. **We eat watermelon on father's day and labor day.**

6. **I wish we could eat watermelon on election day and memorial day, too.**

7. **June 14 is flag day.**

8. **When is labor day?**

NAMES OF HOLIDAYS

Match the holiday names to the pictures.

Flag Day	Mother's Day	Election Day
Thanksgiving	Presidents' Day	New Year's Day

1.

2.

3.

4.

5.

6.

7.–8. Write two sentences that tell what you like to do on a special holiday.

CUMULATIVE REVIEW

Write each sentence correctly.

1. new year's day is on january 1.
2. thanksgiving is on a thursday each year.
3. election day is always on a tuesday.
4. independence day is july 4.
5. Why is father's day always on a sunday?
6. valentine's day is february 14.
7. april fools' day is always april 1.
8. labor day is always on a monday.
9. mother's day is in may.
10. Isn't memorial day in may also?

ABBREVIATIONS

- An **abbreviation** is a short way to write a word.
- Most abbreviations end with a period.
- Abbreviations of proper nouns begin with capital letters.

Write the correct abbreviation for each word.

1.	**March**	**Mr.**	**Mar.**	**Mon.**
2.	**Thursday**	**Thurs.**	**Thsdy.**	**Tues.**
3.	**Saturday**	**St.**	**Satur.**	**Sat.**
4.	**Friday**	**Fr.**	**Feb.**	**Fri.**
5.	**August**	**Ave.**	**Apr.**	**Aug.**

Write each abbreviation correctly.

6.	**feb 20**	11.	**jan 15**
7.	**apr 3**	12.	**sept 5**
8.	**tues, nov 7**	13.	**mon**
9.	**sun**	14.	**wed**
10.	**dec 18**	15.	**oct 30**

ABBREVIATIONS

Read the paragraph. There are 10 days and months named. Write the correct abbreviations for each day and month.

Endings and Beginnings

The school week ends on (1) Friday. The weekend begins on (2) Saturday. It ends on (3) Sunday, and a new school week begins on (4) Monday. In some years, (5) February begins and ends on a (6) Tuesday. On (7) March 21, winter ends and spring begins. On (8) September 22, summer ends and autumn begins. The year ends on (9) December 31. A new year begins on (10) January 1.

CUMULATIVE REVIEW

Write each holiday correctly.

1. **may day**

2. **thanksgiving**

3. **election day**

4. **father's day**

5. **new year's day**

6. **arbor day**

Write each abbreviation correctly.

7. **mar 14**

8. **wed**

9. **oct 10**

10. **sept 2**

11. **fri**

12. **feb 13**

SHOWING OWNERSHIP

- A **possessive noun** shows ownership. It tells what someone or something owns or has.

- When a possessive noun names one person or thing, add an apostrophe (') and *s* to show ownership.

Write the sentences. Circle the possessive noun in each one.

1. Maryland's sunrise is at 6:08 in the morning.

2. Oregon's sunrise is three hours later.

3. My aunt's home is in Portland.

4. Linda's alarm wakes her at seven o'clock.

Write each sentence. Make the noun in ( ) show ownership.

5. (Mr. Rio) job is with NASA.

6. His (spaceship) camera is very good.

7. He took a picture of (Saturn) rings.

8. The (planet) surface was dark.

SHOWING OWNERSHIP

Follow the directions to write the possessive form of each noun.

1. **Earth + apostrophe + *s***

2. **sun + apostrophe + *s***

3. **planet + apostrophe + *s***

4. **moon + apostrophe + *s***

5. **Jupiter + apostrophe + *s***

6. **galaxy + apostrophe + *s***

7. **Neptune + apostrophe + *s***

8.–10. Choose three possessive nouns from above. Write each of them in a sentence of your own.

CUMULATIVE REVIEW

Read the letter. Choose the best way to write each group of underlined words.

(1) **Sat., Nov 10**

Dear John,

In autumn, (2) **the day's get shorter.** We have fewer hours of sunlight. (3) **From june to December,** (4) **each days length** is a bit shorter than the last.

Your friend,
Erika

1. Sat, Nov 10.
   Sat., Nov. 10
   sat., nov. 10

2. the days get shorter.
   the dayses get shorter.
   the days' get shorter.

3. From june to december,
   From June to december,
   From June to December,

4. each day's length
   each day length
   each days' length

PRONOUNS

- A **pronoun** takes the place of a noun.

- *I, you, he, she, it,* and *they* are pronouns.

Write each sentence. Circle the pronouns.

1. **They went to a farm.**

2. **He brought a boa constrictor.**

3. **It dropped to the ground.**

4. **I saw the snake.**

5. **Did Jamie see it, too?**

6. **She saw the snake in the basket.**

Write each sentence, replacing the underlined words with a pronoun.

7. **The girl saw the snake.**

8. **The chickens ran away.**

9. **The egg landed on Jenny's head.**

10. **Did the man feed the pigs?**

PRONOUNS

Write each sentence, replacing the underlined words in each sentence with a pronoun from the box.

I	you	he	she	it	they

1. <u>Pigs</u> have curly tails.
2. <u>The horse</u> likes grass.
3. <u>The students</u> brought lunches.
4. <u>The farmer's wife</u> is afraid of snakes.
5. <u>Jimmy</u> dropped the snake.
6. <u>The two cats</u> are purring.
7. <u>A pig</u> went home with Jimmy.
8. <u>Jenny</u> likes pigs, too.
9. Has <u>Jimmy</u> ever milked a cow?
10. <u>The neighbors</u> came over for dinner.

CUMULATIVE REVIEW

Write each sentence. Draw one line under the naming part and two lines under the telling part.

1. The school bus was full.
2. They visited a farm.
3. Jimmy brought a pet.
4. It was a boa constrictor.
5. The snake ate a mouse.
6. The farmer's wife doesn't like mice, either.

Rewrite each sentence. Replace the underlined word or words with a pronoun.

7. That snake is very long.
8. Jimmy is shorter than the snake.
9. Jenny likes snakes.
10. Why are those people staring?
11. Maybe the pigs are hungry.
12. What does the farmer feed the pigs?

DESCRIBING WORDS

- A **describing word** tells about a noun.
- Some describing words tell about color, size, or shape.

Write each sentence. Circle the describing words that tell about color, size, or shape.

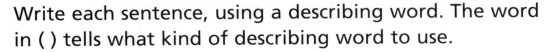

1. **Look at those white clouds.**
2. **She stands near a tall tree.**
3. **That grass is very green.**
4. **The road is straight.**

Write each sentence, using a describing word. The word in ( ) tells what kind of describing word to use.

5. **The sun looks (color).**
6. **The apples are (shape).**
7. **A (size) cow is eating the grass.**

Write *color, size,* or *shape* to tell what each word describes.

8. **thick**

9. **blue**

10. **square**

11. **tall**

DESCRIBING WORDS

Francie took an art class over summer vacation. She wrote a letter to her cousin Tom about it. Francie left out letters of some describing words. Complete each describing word with the correct letters.

Dear Tom,

I like to paint (1) sm__l pictures. I don't like (2) b_g ones. I use lots of colors. My favorites are (3) pur_le and (4) gr__n. I use one brush that is (5) th__k and (6) fl_t. The other one is (7) th_n.

I am also making a (8) r__nd bowl. It is (9) la_ge and (10) whi_e. I can't wait to show you all of the things I have made!

Your cousin,

Francie

CUMULATIVE REVIEW

Write the sentences. Circle the pronoun in each one.

1. Do you like trains?
2. I rode on a train last year.
3. It was fun to travel with Aunt Marie.
4. She took pictures of mountains.
5. Weren't they beautiful?
6. He likes to climb mountains.

Rewrite each sentence, using a describing word. The word in ( ) tells what kind of describing word to use.

7. That table is (shape).
8. The (color) sky looks pretty.
9. The train crossed a (size) river.
10. It was a very (size) train.
11. The leaves on the trees are (color).
12. That clock is (shape).

MORE DESCRIBING WORDS

Write each sentence. Circle the describing words that tell how things taste, smell, sound, or feel.

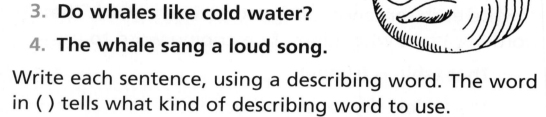

1. **Emily shared her tasty sandwich.**
2. **Does the pond smell fishy?**
3. **Do whales like cold water?**
4. **The whale sang a loud song.**

Write each sentence, using a describing word. The word in ( ) tells what kind of describing word to use.

5. **Maybe whales like (taste) pickles.**
6. **The air smells (smell).**
7. **The water felt (feel) to Emily.**
8. **The whale liked her (sound) voice.**

Write *taste, smell, sound,* or *feel* to tell what each word describes.

9. **squeaky**   11. **salty**
10. **furry**   12. **clean**

MORE DESCRIBING WORDS

1.–10. Read the story. Write the ten words that tell how things taste, smell, sound, or feel. Then write next to each word whether it describes *taste, smell, sound,* or *feel.*

Emily likes the fishy smell of the sea air. She jumps into the cool water. Later, the sand feels hot on her feet. Birds make loud cries. Emily builds a castle out of wet sand. The sun makes her skin feel dry. The sunscreen lotion smells fruity. She hears the crashing sound of the waves. Then she eats a spicy sandwich and some salty pretzels.

CUMULATIVE REVIEW

Write each sentence. Circle each describing word that tells about color, size, or shape.

1. Look at that round pond.
2. The water looks green.
3. Is the whale really blue?
4. It certainly is large.
5. Does it have a pointy tail?
6. It has huge teeth!

Rewrite each sentence, using a describing word. The word in ( ) tells what kind of describing word to use.

7. The whale might like a (taste) cookie.
8. Emily liked the (feel) sand.
9. Whales make (sound) noises.
10. That pond smells (smell).
11. The whale's head felt (feel).
12. (Sound) noises scare whales.

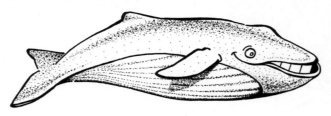

WORDS THAT TELL HOW MANY

- Some describing words tell how many.

Write each sentence. Circle the describing words that tell how many.

1. That dinosaur has many bones.
2. I stopped counting at forty bones.
3. It took me one minute.
4. Some bones were very small.
5. Were all dinosaurs that large?
6. We will leave in fifteen minutes.

Write each sentence, using a describing word that tells how many.

7. That stairway has about (how many) steps.
8. We spent (how many) hours at the museum.
9. We saw (how many) different animals.
10. We will visit again in (how many) weeks.

WORDS THAT TELL HOW MANY

Look at the picture. Then complete each sentence using a word that tells how many of each animal you see.

1. I see (how many) raccoons.

2. There is (how many) cow.

3. I see (how many) skunks.

4. I can count (how many) rabbits.

5. Are there (how many) sheep?

6. I see (how many) elephants.

CUMULATIVE REVIEW

Write each sentence. Circle the word that tells how many, and draw one line under nouns that name more than one.

1. Forty children went to the museum.

2. A few teachers had cameras.

3. The display shows two frogs on a log.

4. Some geese were swimming in the pond.

Write each sentence, using a describing word. The word or words in ( ) tell what kind of describing word to use.

5. The museum has (how many) dinosaurs.

6. The dinosaur's bones feel (feel).

7. (How many) visitors saw the big dinosaur.

8. It was (sound) in the lunchroom.

9. My tuna sandwich smelled (smell).

10. The chips tasted (taste).

WORDS THAT COMPARE

Skill Reminder

- A describing word that ends with **-er** compares one thing with one other thing.

- A describing word that ends with **-est** compares one thing with two or more other things.

Write each sentence. Circle the describing words that compare.

1. Today is warmer than yesterday.

2. That oak is the tallest tree on the block.

3. Today is the longest day of the year.

4. My hat is wider than your hat.

5. North winds are the coldest of all.

6. A sunflower is taller than a lily.

7. Pencils are longer than pieces of chalk.

8. Is Ali the smallest girl in our class?

Write each sentence. Choose the correct answer in ( ).

9. This mountain is the (bigger/biggest) of all.

10. Are you (older/oldest) than I am?

WORDS THAT COMPARE

Write each sentence. Choose the correct word in ( ).

1. Black is the (darker/darkest) crayon of all.

2. Yellow is (lighter/lightest) than black.

3. Your chalk is (thicker/thickest) than my chalk.

4. Do raindrops fall (faster/fastest) than snowflakes?

5. Last year we had the (deeper/deepest) snow ever.

6. The snowman is (taller/tallest) than the girl.

7. This is the (colder/coldest) winter we have had in years.

8. Who is the (shorter/shortest) person in your family?

9. Mother is (shorter/shortest) than Father.

10. Whose bike is the (faster/fastest) one of all?

CUMULATIVE REVIEW

Choose the best way to write each group of underlined words.

Ali drew a lake (1) **for mrs Frye.** Next, she drew a very large umbrella for Ira Baker. The umbrella was (2) **largest than the lake.** (3) **Ali used four colors** for the umbrella. For the North Wind, Ali needed (4) **many piece of white chalk.**

1. for mrs. frye
   for mrs frye.
   for Mrs. Frye.
   No mistake

2. largest than the Lake.
   larger than the lake.
   larger of all.
   No mistake

3. ali used for colors
   ali used four color
   Ali used for color
   No mistake

4. many pieces of white chalk.
   many Pieces of white Chalk.
   many pieces of white chalks.
   No mistake

VERBS THAT TELL ABOUT NOW

Skill Reminder

- An **action verb** tells what someone or something does.

- A verb can tell about an action that is happening **now**.

Write each sentence. Circle the verb.

1. The sun shines in the sky.

2. Children walk to school.

3. Mothers chat on the path.

4. Some people talk.

5. The dog watches everyone.

Write the sentences. Choose the verb from the box that best completes each sentence.

| babbles | waves | wipes |

6. The park worker ___ the bench dry.

7. A little baby ___ quietly in his stroller.

8. One friend ___ to another.

VERBS THAT TELL ABOUT NOW

Complete each sentence by adding a verb. Look at the picture for ideas.

1. **Mist ___ over the park.**

2. **Some people ___ their dogs.**

3. **The old man ___ on the white bench.**

4. **Friends ___ at the park.**

5. **The girl ___ on the path.**

6.–8. Write three sentences of your own about the park. Use a verb from the box in each sentence.

relax	run	talks

CUMULATIVE REVIEW

Write each sentence. Use the correct word in ( ).

1. Stewart Park is (smaller/smallest) than City Park.

2. City Park is the (cleaner/cleanest) park of all.

3. The sidewalk is (broader/broadest) than my street.

4. Is City Park (larger/largest) than Central Park?

5. It is the (greener/greenest) place I know.

6. Which park is the (bigger/biggest)?

Write each sentence. Circle the verb.

7. Some children fly kites in the park.

8. The kites swoop above the trees.

9. One red kite dives down.

10. It nearly hits the sidewalk.

11. Then it leaps up again.

12. The wind carries it higher.

13. The sun shines in their eyes.

14. They pull on the kite's string.

AGREEMENT

Write the verb from each sentence. Then write *one* or *more than one* to show how many the naming part tells about.

1. **The wind blows.**

2. **Some birds hop by.**

3. **Kids play in the park.**

Write each sentence. Use the correct verb in ( ).

4. **The badge (shine/shines) in the sun.**

5. **I (put/puts) my key on a rock.**

6. **The friends (hide/hides).**

7. **A black bird (swoop/swoops) down.**

8. **The grown-ups (laugh/laughs).**

AGREEMENT

Write each sentence, using the correct form of a verb from the box.

| jump | meet | ride | skate | throw | walk | sleep |

(1) Every Saturday, my friends ___ near the ball field. (2) I ___ my bike. (3) Jeff ___ his ball up high. (4) Suki ___ rope. (5) The Johnson twins ___ . (6) Then we ___ home for dinner. (7) I ___ well because I am tired.

8.–9. Write two sentences about the picture. Use the verbs below.

| play | plays |

CUMULATIVE REVIEW

Read each sentence. Write the verb.

1. **Mysteries thrill Lan.**
2. **That bird steals everything.**
3. **People lose their jewelry.**
4. **The police chief mutters.**
5. **Jeff solves the puzzle.**

Write each sentence. Use the correct verb in ( ).

6. **You (like/likes) shiny things.**
7. **Some birds (learn/learns) easily.**
8. **Miss Rosa (train/trains) her bird.**
9. **Dynah (know/knows) several words.**
10. **Her speech (surprise/surprises) everyone.**

PAST-TENSE VERBS

- A verb can tell about action in the **past**.
- Add **-ed** to most verbs to tell about the past.

Read the sentences below. Write each verb that tells about the past.

1. Curtis delivered the mail.

2. He pushed a letter into the box.

3. Mrs. Martin opened the letter.

4. Curtis hauled a big sack.

5. He pulled letters from the sack.

Write each sentence. Use the correct form of the verb in ( ).

6. One letter (flutter) to the ground.

7. Curtis (pick) it up.

8. Then he (rest) on a bench.

9. Curtis (enjoy) his job.

10. He (walk) in rain or shine.

PAST-TENSE VERBS

1.–5. This letter has verbs that tell about now. Rewrite the letter. Make each verb tell about the past.

Dear Dennis,

   In May I visit my aunts. They treat me to a trip to the circus. We watch the acrobats. Some clowns climb up on a bike. I enjoy the animal acts.

Your cousin,

Sarah

6.–8. Write three sentences to tell about something you did. Use verbs that tell about the past.

CUMULATIVE REVIEW

Write each sentence. Draw a line under the verbs that tell about now and two lines under the verbs that tell about the past.

1. Mrs. Martin addressed a letter.
2. She writes to her cousin every week.
3. Donny licks the stamp.
4. Curtis sorted the letters.

Write each sentence, using the form of the verb in ( ) to tell about the past.

5. He (deliver) them to the post office.
6. One man (sort) some letters.
7. The letters (seem) ready.

Write each sentence. Use the correct form of the verb in ( ).

8. A woman (run/runs) the postage meter.
9. Postal workers (read/reads) fast.
10. Curtis (place/places) the letters in his sack.

AM, IS, ARE, WAS, WERE

- Some verbs do not show action. They tell what someone or something is like.
- *Am, is,* and *are* tell about now.
- *Was* and *were* tell about the past.

Write the verb in each sentence.

1. **The family was in the city.**

2. **Max's parents are city workers.**

3. **I am Max's next-door neighbor.**

Write each sentence, using the correct verb in ( ).

4. **Those drumsticks (is/are) a gift.**

5. **A real drummer (was/were) here.**

6. **He (is/are) a friend of Max's.**

7. **I (was/were) on the steps with Max.**

8. **The band members (was/were) nearby.**

AM, IS, ARE, WAS, WERE

Write the correct verb for each word. Use *am, is, are, was,* or *were.*

NOW	PAST
1. I	2. I
3. you	4. you
5. she	6. she
7. we	8. we
9. they	10. they

11.–12. Choose two verbs from the exercise above. Write two sentences using one of the verbs you chose in each sentence.

CUMULATIVE REVIEW

Write the verb in each sentence. Then write if it tells about the *past* or *now.*

1. Max drums on some boxes.

2. The twins like their new hats.

3. The hats are very pretty.

4. Mother ordered the hats.

5. They were a birthday gift.

6. It is sunny outside.

Rewrite each sentence. Use the correct verb in ( ).

7. I (am/is) Max's friend.

8. He (was/were) in my class.

9. Now we (is/are) in a band.

10. Max (is/are) a good singer.

11. I (was/were) a guitar player.

12. The people (was/were) happy to hear our music.

HAS, HAVE, HAD

- *Has* and *have* tell about now.
- *Had* tells about the past.

Write the verb in each sentence.

1. **Max had a wonderful hat.**

2. **That hat has silver bells.**

3. **I have a hat with red beads.**

4. **We have to wear hats outside.**

Rewrite each sentence. Use the correct verb in ( ).

5. **This hat (has/have) a long history.**

6. **My grandfather (have/had) it first.**

7. **He (have/had) a job as a charro.**

8. **My grandparents (has/have) a restaurant.**

HAS, HAVE, HAD

Write the correct verb for each word. Use *has, have,* or *had.*

NOW	PAST
1. I	2. I
3. you	4. you
5. it	6. it
7. we	8. we
9. they	10. they

11.–12. Choose two verbs from the exercise above. Write two sentences using one of the verbs you chose in each sentence.

Choose the best way to write each group of underlined words.

I work as a charro. (1) <u>A charro am a Mexican cowboy.</u>
(2) <u>Charros have a difficult job.</u> They ride horses. (3)
<u>They ropes cows.</u> I like my job. (4) <u>It be lots of fun.</u>

1. A charro be a mexican cowboy.

   A charro is a Mexican cowboy.

   No mistake

2. Charros has a difficult job.

   A charro have a difficult job.

   No mistake

3. They rope cows.

   They roping cows.

   No mistake

4. It are lots of fun.

   It is lots of fun.

   No mistake

SEE, GIVE, SAW, GAVE

Write each sentence. Draw one line under verbs that tell about now and two lines under verbs that tell about the past.

1. Montigue sees a scary cat.
2. He gave the mice a piece of cheese.
3. The mice give him a bottle.
4. I saw Montigue's new home.
5. He gives his neighbors a hand.

Rewrite each sentence. Make each verb tell about now.

6. Montigue saw a sailboat.
7. A mouse gave him some help.
8. Soon the animals saw land.

SEE, GIVE, SAW, GAVE

Rewrite each sentence. Make each verb tell about the past.

1. **Montigue sees the big waves.**
2. **The waves give him a scare.**
3. **The mice see a way out.**
4. **He gives the cat a treat.**
5. **The birds see fish in the ocean.**
6. **Montigue gives the boy a pail.**

7.–11. Rewrite the story. Make each verb tell about now.

The mole saw sailors. The sailors saw him, too. A cat gave him a swat. Montigue saw a hole. He gave a cheer.

CUMULATIVE REVIEW

Write the verb from each sentence. Then write whether it tells about the *past* or *now*.

1. **The mole had a good idea.**

2. **Soon the mice see land.**

3. **They give a loud cheer.**

4. **They gave Montigue a ride.**

5. **Now he has a new home.**

Write each sentence. Use the correct verb found in ( ).

6. **Montigue still (have/has) the bottle.**

7. **The mole (give/gives) it to the mouse museum.**

8. **Visitors (see/sees) it every day.**

COME, RUN, CAME, RAN

Skill Reminder

- The verbs **come** and **run** tell about now.
- Add *–s* to *come* and *run* to tell what *he, she, it,* or a noun that names one person or thing does.
- The verbs **came** and **ran** tell about the past.

Write each sentence. Draw one line under verbs that tell about now and two lines under the verbs that tell about the past.

1. **A bus comes down the street.**

2. **Some children run on the sidewalk.**

3. **I nearly ran into that sign.**

4. **My brother came along with me.**

5. **Tourists come here often.**

Rewrite each sentence. Make each verb tell about now.

6. **Taxis came along every hour.**

7. **The tourists ran for a cab.**

8. **My father ran very quickly.**

COME, RUN, CAME, RAN

Rewrite each sentence. Make each verb tell about the past.

1. A dinosaur comes by on a bike.

2. The bike path runs downhill.

3. The bike's wheels run faster and faster.

4. They come by my house.

5. I run after them.

6. They run very fast!

7.–11. Rewrite the story. Make each verb tell about now.

A jogger ran by. Two dogs ran with him. The three of them came past my car. The black dog came first. He ran the fastest.

CUMULATIVE REVIEW

Write the verb in each sentence. Then write whether it tells about the *past* or *now*.

1. A train runs faster than a car.
2. The car came in third.
3. Many people see the race.
4. The bike ran slowest of all.
5. We give the airplane a medal.

Write each sentence. Use the correct verb in ( ).

6. The trains (run/runs) on tracks.
7. The conductor (come/comes) along.
8. Aaron (give/gives) her his ticket.
9. The food cart (come/came) by.
10. Erik (run/ran) to get a drink.

GO, DO, WENT, DID

- The verbs **go** and **do** tell about now.
- Add –es to go and do when the naming part of a sentence is he, she, it, or a noun that names one person or thing.
- The verbs **went** and **did** tell about the past.

Write each sentence. Draw one line under verbs that tell about now and two lines under verbs that tell about the past.

1. **Abuela does funny things.**

2. **The two of us went for a walk.**

3. **Sometimes we go to the park.**

4. **Today we did just that.**

5. **I often do exciting things with her.**

Rewrite each sentence. Make each verb tell about now.

6. **The two friends went to the park.**

7. **Abuela did some wonderful tricks.**

8. **The day went by quickly.**

GO, DO, WENT, DID

Write each sentence. Use the correct verb in ( ).

1. My grandmother (go/goes) to the park.

2. The birds (do/does) happy dances.

3. Some dogs (go/goes) past quickly.

4. My dad (do/does) the dishes.

5. My mother (go/goes) upstairs to relax.

6. My brothers (do/does) their homework.

7.–11. Rewrite the story. Make each verb tell about the past.

   Abuela does tricks. Rosalba goes into the air. Birds go past her. Some go around her head. They do a dance.

CUMULATIVE REVIEW

Copy the chart. Write the correct forms of each verb. The first one has been done for you.

VERB	NOW	PAST
1. come	come, comes	came
2. do		
3. run		
4. go		
5. see		

Rewrite each sentence. Make each verb tell about the past.

6. I go to the park.

7. Abuela comes with me.

8. We do this every Saturday.

9. Then we go to a movie.

10. I do my chores.

HELPING VERBS

- A **helping verb** works with the main verb to tell about an action.
- *Has, have,* and *had* can be used as helping verbs.

Write each sentence. Underline the main verb. Circle the helping verb.

1. Ruth Law had dreamed about flying.
2. She has planned this trip well.
3. Mechanics have prepared the plane.
4. The little plane has lifted off.
5. Few people had believed in Ruth.

Write each sentence. Use the correct helping verb in ( ).

6. The plane (has/have) reached Hornell, New York.
7. Crowds (has/have) greeted Ruth Law.
8. Ruth (has/have) rested for an hour.
9. Some mechanics (has/have) refueled the plane.
10. The plane (has/have) flown into the sky.

HELPING VERBS

Read the paragraph. Rewrite each sentence, adding the helping verb *have* or *has.*

(1) **Ruth Law left Chicago.** (2) **She landed in Hornell, New York.** (3) **People in Hornell treated her to lunch.** (4) **Her little plane traveled to the next town.** (5) **Spectators cheered her arrival.**

6.–8. Write three sentences using *have* or *has* with each verb in the box.

talked	eaten	tried

CUMULATIVE REVIEW

Write each sentence. Underline the main verb. Circle the helping verb.

1. I have flown on a plane before.
2. Valerie has fallen asleep.
3. Gregg and his dog have gone for a walk.
4. They had tried to get tickets.
5. The concert has sold out.

Write each sentence. Use the correct helping verb in ( ).

6. Air travel (has/have) changed.
7. Early pilots (has/have) led the way.
8. My grandmother (has/have) traveled in a helicopter.
9. My parents (has/have) soared in jets.
10. Ross (has/have) ridden on a train.

CONTRACTIONS

- A **contraction** is a short way to write two words.
- An apostrophe (') takes the place of the missing letter or letters.

Write the two words that make up the contraction found in each sentence.

1. **The planets don't move slowly.**

2. **The moon isn't a plane.**

3. **We haven't traveled to Saturn.**

4. **Mars wasn't really red.**

5. **I didn't know that!**

Rewrite each sentence. Use a contraction in place of the underlined word or words.

6. **You <u>cannot</u> see Pluto without a telescope.**

7. **Tiny planets <u>are not</u> easy to spot.**

8. **We <u>do not</u> know much about Pluto.**

CONTRACTIONS

Write a contraction for each pair of words.

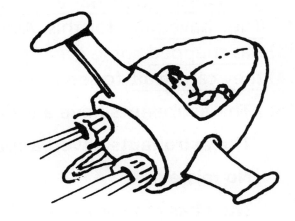

1. **had not**

2. **has not**

3. **were not**

4. **is not**

5. **did not**

6. **should not**

7. **have not**

8. **do not**

9. **would not**

10. **was not**

Rewrite the paragraph. Use a contraction in place of the underlined word or words.

(11) **Do not** plan a trip to Venus. It (12) **is not** very comfortable. You (13) **cannot** breathe there. Venus (14) **does not** have much oxygen. That is why we (15) **have not** traveled there.

CUMULATIVE REVIEW

Choose the best way to write each group of underlined words.

(1) <u>The astronauts has a great view</u> of the Earth.
(2) <u>They have plan</u> for this. Astronaut Perkins
(3) <u>has snapped</u> some great pictures. On Earth,
(4) <u>they cant wait</u> to see the photos.

1. **The astronauts have a great view**

   The astronauts haved a great view

   No mistake

2. **They has planned**

   They have planned

   No mistake

3. **snap**

   has snap

   No mistake

4. **They cant' wait**

   they can't wait

   No mistake

Additional Practice

ADDITIONAL PRACTICE
Sentences

Read each group of words. Write *yes* if the words make a sentence. Write *no* if the words do not make a sentence.

Example:

I like to play soccer.

yes

1. practice on Saturdays

2. lost the first game

3. My sister helps me.

4. We practice every day.

5. made a goal

6. my sister and I

7. I thank my sister.

8. Pete is our best player.

9. Teresa and Gillian

10. My dad comes to our games.

Naming Part of a Sentence

Write each sentence. Underline the naming part.

Example:

The dogs like music.
The dogs like music.

1. **The school has a band.**

2. **Rover leads the band.**

3. **The flutes are the softest.**

4. **Jack plays the trumpet.**

5. **His friend plays the tuba.**

6. **They practice every day.**

7. **Pepe is the smallest dog of all.**

8. **The band marches outside.**

9. **Fido leads the other dogs.**

10. **The parade begins at noon.**

Writing What is your favorite animal? Write a sentence about the animal. Underline the naming part of your sentence.

ADDITIONAL PRACTICE
Joining Naming Parts

Complete the sentences by joining the naming parts.
Then write the sentences.

Example:

Michael cut the grass.
Mary cut the grass.
Michael and Mary cut the grass.

1. **Eli made the beds.**

   Miguel made the beds.

   ___ and ___ made the beds.

2. **Tony made sandwiches.**

   Jan made sandwiches.

   ___ and ___ made sandwiches.

3. **Patty poured milk.**

   Tessa poured milk.

   ___ and ___ poured milk.

4. **Dan washed the dog.**

   Cindy washed the dog.

   ___ and ___ washed the dog.

Telling Part of a Sentence

Write each sentence. Underline the telling part.

Example:

We return bottles to the store.
We __return bottles to the store__.

1. Friends help us.

2. Molly saves plastic containers.

3. The newspapers are in boxes.

4. Frank collects aluminum cans.

5. The neighbors give us glass bottles.

6. We sort the trash.

7. Mom drives to the recycling center.

8. We dump trash into bins.

ADDITIONAL PRACTICE
Joining Telling Parts

Join the telling parts of each pair of sentences.
Use the word *and*. Write new sentences.

Example:

Keena adds.
Keena subtracts.
Keena adds and subtracts.

1. **Seth reads.**

   Seth writes.

2. **Brian listens to his teacher.**

   Brian does his homework.

3. **Amy prints spelling words.**

   Amy checks her paper.

4. **Mike writes a story.**

   Mike draws pictures.

5. **Maria raises her hand.**

   Maria tells the answer.

Word Order

Write each group of words in the correct order.

Example:

plays Reba tennis.
Reba plays tennis.

1. to be wants She a star.

2. Reba day practices every.

3. she wins Sometimes games.

4. games Sometimes loses she.

5. with other children plays tennis Reba.

6. better is getting Reba.

7. started Nate tennis lessons.

8. fast run He can.

ADDITIONAL PRACTICE
Statements

Read each statement. Find the statements that have mistakes. Write those statements correctly.

Example:

ben is my friend
Ben is my friend.

1. he uses a wheelchair

2. at school Ben is in my class

3. we study together

4. Mom takes us to the movies.

5. sometimes Ben needs my help

6. then I open doors for him

7. Ben has a lot of stamps.

8. we like to trade stamps.

Questions

Write each sentence correctly.

Example:

what is your penguin's name
What is your penguin's name?

1. my penguin's name is Tuffy

2. where did you get her

3. does your baby brother like her

4. can he play with Tuffy

5. I pretend Tuffy is real

6. would you like to hear her talk

7. why are penguins mostly black and white

8. is Tuffy a stuffed animal

9. when can I hold her

10. my mom loves penguins

Writing Write two questions about penguins. Share your questions by reading them to a classmate. Work together to find the answers.

ADDITIONAL PRACTICE
Exclamations and Commands

Read each sentence. Is it an exclamation or a command? Write the sentences correctly.

Example:

Stay near shore
Stay near shore.

1. Bring your bathing suit
2. Hooray, we're going to the beach
3. Invite a friend
4. We'll have lots of fun
5. I'm so hot
6. Jump into the water
7. Don't splash
8. Here come the waves
9. Wow, there's a shark
10. What an adventure we had

End Marks

Write each sentence correctly. Add a period, a question mark, or an exclamation point.

Example:

Lee is my good friend
Lee is my good friend.

1. **Do you know why I like him**
2. **He shares his toys with me**
3. **He tells me funny jokes**
4. **How he makes me laugh**
5. **What fun we have together**
6. **Do you have a special friend**
7. **Tell me your friend's name**
8. **Is his name Tom**

Writing Write one question and one statement about a game you like.

Practice

ADDITIONAL PRACTICE
Nouns

Read each sentence. Write the noun or nouns. For each noun, write whether it names a person, an animal, a place, or a thing.

Example:

These friends help in their neighborhood.
friends—people
neighborhood—place

1. Some children work in a garden.

2. The man shows what to do.

3. A girl plants corn.

4. She uses a shovel and a hoe.

5. A boy waters the daisies.

6. Even the squirrel helps!

7. It picks up nuts from the ground.

8. Then it runs up the tree.

Special Names and Titles of People

Write each sentence correctly. Add capital letters and periods where they are needed.

Example:

mr davis has an orange tree in his yard.
Mr. Davis has an orange tree in his yard.

1. Look, mrs sanchez has a watering can.

2. What did alexandra bring?

3. Yes, dr roberts brought a shovel.

4. He and mrs grove brought the tree.

5. We can plant it in ms handy's yard.

6. Then jennifer will have fresh oranges.

ADDITIONAL PRACTICE
Names of Special Animals and Places

A. Choose the correct word to complete each sentence. Write the sentences.

Example:

Our fish is named (goldy, Goldy).
Our fish is named Goldy.

1. **We went to (san francisco, San Francisco).**

2. **It is in (california, California).**

3. **We brought our cat, (sandy, Sandy).**

B. Write each sentence correctly. Add capital letters where they are needed.

Example:

My dog, frisky, came from seattle.
My dog, Frisky, came from Seattle.

1. **Our dog, peke, is very cute.**

2. **He comes from the city of peking.**

3. **It is a city in china.**

Names of Days, Months, and Holidays

A. Read each sentence. Write the name of the day, month, or holiday that is written correctly.

Example:

Our county fair is held in (august, August).
August

1. Each year, we go on a field trip in (April, april).

2. On (tuesday, Tuesday), we went to a farm.

3. We bought seeds for (may, May) flowers.

4. I planted my seeds on (wednesday, Wednesday).

5. I gave the plant to my mother on (Mother's Day, mother's day).

6. In (June, june) the plant had big flowers.

7. They were in bloom on the (fourth of july, Fourth of July).

ADDITIONAL PRACTICE

B. Write each sentence correctly. Add capital letters where they are needed.

Example:

It snowed on new year's day.
It snowed on New Year's Day.

1. On monday, Mr. Quinn yelled at the dog.

2. On tuesday, he slammed his door.

3. He was grouchy all through january.

4. On valentine's day, he got three valentines.

5. He started smiling more in february.

6. He wore a tall hat on presidents' day.

7. He laughed out loud in march.

8. He won a blue ribbon in july.

Writing Write about your favorite holiday. Use capital letters where they are needed.

Titles of Books

A. Write each sentence correctly. Add capital letters where they are needed.

Example:

Have you read <u>henry and mudge</u>?
*Have you read <u>**Henry and Mudge**</u>?*

1. I liked reading <u>**the stinky cheese man**</u>.

2. Another funny book is <u>**old turtle's baseball stories**</u>.

3. If you like baseball, you'll like <u>**frank and ernest play ball**</u>.

B. Write these book titles correctly.

Example:

time of wonder

*<u>**Time of Wonder**</u>*

4. chicken soup and rice

5. the bicycle man

6. peter and the wolf

ADDITIONAL PRACTICE
Plural Nouns

A. Choose the correct noun in each sentence.
Write the noun.

Example:

Our two (friend, friends) are getting ready for the carnival.

friends

1. The carnival begins with a parade of many (clown, clowns).

2. The first clown is riding on an (elephant, elephants).

3. Some (child, children) are in the parade.

4. They are carrying (pets, pet).

5. Two baby (fox, foxes) are in a cage.

6. Some (men, man) are riding horses.

B. Make each underlined noun mean more than one. Write the sentences.

Example:

I have been to two <u>circus</u>.
I have been to two circuses.

1. The circus has many <u>clown</u>.

2. Most clowns have big <u>foot</u>.

3. Many <u>dog</u> do tricks.

4. Big dogs come out of little <u>box</u>.

5. The lion tamer has many <u>lion</u>.

6. Three <u>man</u> are jugglers.

7. Two <u>woman</u> ride horses bareback.

8. All the <u>tiger</u> come out last.

ADDITIONAL PRACTICE
Pronouns

A. Write the pronoun that can take the place of the underlined word or words.

Example:

<u>The animals</u> watch. He   She   It   They
They

1. <u>**Mom**</u> **was sleeping.** He   She   It   They

2. <u>**Dad**</u> **was in the boat.** He   She   It   They

3. <u>**An owl**</u> **hoots.** He   She   It   They

4. <u>**Two mice**</u> **run by.** He   She   It   They

5. <u>**Sam and Esme**</u> **yell.** He   She   It   They

B. Read each sentence. Think of a pronoun for the underlined word or words. Write the new sentence.

Example:

<u>Ari</u> likes to go camping.
He likes to go camping.

1. <u>**Sara**</u> **built a campfire.**

2. <u>**James**</u> **told a story.**

3. <u>**The story**</u> **was scary.**

Describing Words

A. Look at the picture. Then write each sentence. Circle the describing word. Draw a line under the noun it tells about.

Example:

There are five snakes in the parade.

There are (five) <u>snakes</u> in the parade.

1. They wear tiny hats.

2. Meg's hat has a square shape.

3. Max has a yellow belly.

4. Sal has a round balloon.

5. Fred blows a loud horn.

ADDITIONAL PRACTICE

B. Look at the picture on page 189. Use words from the box to complete each sentence. Write the sentence.

little	bumpy	smooth
square	sweet	hissing

Example:

Sam is holding a ___ sign.
Sam is holding a __square__ sign.

1. **Meg is pulling some ___ bells.**

2. **The ___ ground makes the bells jingle.**

3. **The apple tastes ___.**

4. **The snakes make ___ sounds.**

5. **They all have ___ skin.**

Writing List some words that describe apples. Then use one of the words in a sentence about an apple.

Describing Words That Compare

Choose the correct describing word.
Write the sentences.

Example:

Some dinosaurs were (strong, stronger) than others.

Some dinosaurs were <u>stronger</u> than others.

1. Some had (sharper, sharpest) teeth than others.

2. The Brachiosaurus was one of the (large, largest) dinosaurs of all.

3. It was (taller, tallest) than 40 feet.

4. Its front legs were (longer, longest) than its back ones.

5. It could reach the (higher, highest) leaves.

ADDITIONAL PRACTICE
Verbs That Tell About Now

Choose a verb from the box to complete each sentence.
Add *s* to the verb if you need to. Write the sentence.

enjoy	tell	like
help	paint	sew
work	sing	read

Example:

My class ___ to put on plays.
My class <u>likes</u> to put on plays.

1. Each child ___ with the work.

2. Some people ___ the costumes.

3. Others ___ the background.

4. We all ___ very hard.

5. Our play ___ about dinosaurs.

6. We ___ working together.

7. Ms. Arnold ___ our lines with us.

Verbs That Tell About the Past

Find the verb in each sentence. Make it tell about the past. Then write the new sentence.

Example:

My family visits the zoo.
My family visited the zoo.

1. We watch the animals.

2. The monkeys climb ropes.

3. The seals jump off rocks.

4. My sister wants to buy a balloon.

5. Later, we munch on popcorn.

6. Two apes play with a tire.

7. Dad talks to a parrot!

8. We laugh all the way home.

ADDITIONAL PRACTICE
Is, Am, Are

Choose *is*, *am*, or *are* to finish each sentence.
Then write the sentence.

Example:

The state fair ___ fun.
The state fair is fun.

1. **The clowns ___ silly.**

2. **That cowgirl ___ brave.**

3. **I ___ so excited!**

4. **Some animals ___ loud.**

5. **My brother ___ excited, too.**

6. **Dad's apple pie ___ yummy!**

7. **I ___ thrilled to be at the fair.**

8. **Rosa's pet pig ___ a winner.**

Writing Think about a person or an animal you know well. Write sentences about what he or she is like. Check to be sure you have used the verbs *is, am,* and *are* correctly.

Was, Were

Choose *was* or *were* to finish each sentence. Then write the sentence.

Example:

J. Mouse ___ happy.

J. Mouse <u>was</u> happy.

1. **Two presents ___ on the table.**

2. **One gift ___ pretty.**

3. **The other one ___ ugly.**

4. **Both boxes ___ big.**

5. **The mouse's eyes ___ big.**

6. **J. Mouse ___ sad.**

7. **The box ___ empty!**

8. **The two mice ___ good friends.**

ADDITIONAL PRACTICE
Has, Have, Had

Choose *has*, *have*, or *had* to finish each sentence. Then write the sentence.

Example:

Last year, the boys ___ a contest.
Last year, the boys <u>had</u> a contest.

1. **This year, the girls and boys ___ another contest.**

2. **The children ___ board games to play.**

3. **Monica and Darrell ___ a checkers set.**

4. **Today Mr. Wills ___ dominoes.**

5. **Last year, two boys ___ a prize for the winner.**

6. **Yesterday, one girl ___ an idea for a new prize.**

7. **Today Mr. Wills ___ a big blue ribbon.**

8. **Now all the children ___ fun playing board games.**

Writing Think about a game you have played many times. Write two sentences about the game. Try to use *has, have,* or *had* in your sentences.

Helping Verbs

Write each sentence. Circle the helping verb.

Example:

We had left home early.
We (had) left home early.

1. Now we have arrived at the camp.

2. Tom and Bill have unloaded the car.

3. Mr. Green had shopped for food the day before.

4. Bob has gathered firewood.

5. Something strange has happened.

6. A spaceship has landed nearby!

ADDITIONAL PRACTICE
See and *Give*

Read each sentence. Make the underlined verb tell about the past. Write the sentence.

Example:

Shayla <u>sees</u> a picture in a cookbook.
Shayla saw a picture in a cookbook.

1. She <u>sees</u> a recipe, too.

2. She <u>gives</u> the book to her mother.

3. The recipe <u>gives</u> a list of things needed.

4. Shayla's mother <u>gives</u> her some help.

5. Later, Kim <u>sees</u> huge cookies.

6. Shayla <u>gives</u> her a monster cookie.

Come and Run

A. Choose the correct verb. Write the sentence.

Example:

We (come, comes) to the park to work.
We come to the park to work.

1. **The families (come, comes) to help clean up the park.**

2. **She (come, comes) to pick up litter.**

3. **Dad (come, comes) to paint.**

4. **My dog (run, runs) after the bird.**

5. **Two birds (run, runs) away.**

B. Change the verb in each sentence above so that it tells about the past. Write the sentence.

Example:

We come to the park to work.
We came to the park to work.

ADDITIONAL PRACTICE
Go and *Do*

A. Read each sentence. Write the correct verb.

Example:

The wasps ___ their work.
do   does
The wasps do their work.

   1. **The wasps ___ to their nest under the roof.**
     go   goes

   2. **They ___ many things.**
     do   does

   3. **One wasp ___ the hardest job.**
     do   does

   4. **Other wasps ___ for food.**
     go   goes

B. Change the verb in each sentence above so that it tells about the past. Write the sentence.

Example:

The wasps do their work.
The wasps did their work.

Agreement

Choose the correct verb. Write the sentence.

Example:

Sea otters (live, lives) in the ocean.
Sea otters live in the ocean.

1. They (eats, eat) crabs and shellfish.

2. A sea otter hardly ever (comes, come) to the shore.

3. It even (sleep, sleeps) in the water.

4. Sea otters (need, needs) their fur.

5. Sometimes sticky oil (cover, covers) an otter's fur.

6. Some people (cleans, clean) the oil from the fur.

7. Ships (spill, spills) oil into the ocean.

Writing What kinds of animals live in the ocean? Choose one animal. Write a few sentences about the animal. Check to be sure that your verbs agree with the naming parts of your sentences.

ADDITIONAL PRACTICE
Contractions

A. Read each sentence. Write the contraction for the two words in parentheses ( ).

Example:

Some pandas (do not) look like bears.
don't

1. **People (did not) want the pandas to die.**

2. **Pandas (are not) easy to keep in zoos.**

3. **Giant pandas (do not) live without bamboo to eat.**

4. **Saving pandas (is not) easy.**

B. Read each sentence. Write the two words that make up the underlined contraction.

Example:

The zoo <u>wasn't</u> crowded.
was not

1. **I <u>didn't</u> see the zoo's panda.**

2. **The shy panda <u>isn't</u> outside.**

To, Too, Two

A. Write the correct word for each sentence.

Example:

A honey guide flew (too, to) a branch.
to

1. **A honey guide and a ratel are (to, two) animal partners.**

2. **The honey guide flies (to, two) a bees' nest but can't open it.**

3. **It looks (to, too) the ratel for help.**

B. Complete each sentence with <u>to</u>, <u>too</u>, or <u>two</u>. Write the sentences.

Example:

The ___ animals help each other.
The <u>two</u> animals help each other.

1. **The ratel goes ___ the nest.**

2. **The honey guide eats from the nest, ___.**

3. **The ___ animals have a sweet friendship.**

ADDITIONAL PRACTICE

There, Their, They're

Read each sentence. Write the correct word.

Example:

Elephants grow for most of (there, their) lives.
their

1. Many elephants make (their, there) homes in Africa.

2. (They're, There) the largest land animals.

3. Young elephants live with (their, there) mothers.

4. (There, They're) watched over by the whole herd.

5. Hunters kill elephants for (their, there) ivory tusks.

6. Elephants (they're, there) may be in danger.

7. Some countries (they're, there) have passed laws.

8. (Their, They're) trying to save the elephants.

A

Abbreviations, 118–120

Additional practice, 169–204

Address (envelope), 59

Adjectives. *See* **Describing words.**

Agreement, 142–144, 201

B

Book report, 68–69

Book title, 185

C

Capitalization
  days of the week,
    110–111, 183–184
  first word of sentence,
    79–81, 82–84, 170,
    176–177
  holidays, 115–117,
    183–184
  months of the year,
    112–114, 183–184
  names of special animals
    and places, 106–108,
    182
  special names of people,
    103–105, 181
  titles of books, 185
  titles of people,
    103–105, 181

Come and ***run***, 157–159,
  199

Command. *See* **Sentences.**

Comparatives, 136–138, 191

Contractions, 166–168, 202

D

Describing words
  adding to sentences, 127,
    190
  comparing with *-er* or
    -est, 136–138, 191
  definition of, 127
  size, shape, color,
    number, 130–132, 189
  taste, smell, sound,
    feel, 127–128, 189

Details, 11, 13, 14–15,
  19–21, 24–25

Drafting, 2, 8, 12, 16, 20, 24

E

Effective Sentences, 22–25

Elements of handwriting
  common errors, 39
  cursive letters, 32–33, 35
  manuscript letters,
    30–31, 34
  position, size, stroke, 38
  shape, 36
  spacing, 37

End marks. *See* Sentences,
  punctuation of.
Envelope (address), 59
Exclamation. *See* Sentences.
Explanations, 66–67

Focus/Ideas, 6–9

Go and *do*, 160–162, 200
Grammar, 77–168
  See also Additional
  practice.

Handwriting, 30–39
  See also Elements of
  handwriting.
Helping verbs, 163–165, 197
How-to paragraph, 72–73

I, 124–125
Information paragraph,
  64–65
Invitation, 56–57

Joining naming parts of
  sentences, 172
Joining telling parts of
  sentences, 174
Journal, 3, 48

Letter, friendly, 54–55

Mechanics
  apostrophe, 166–168, 202
  comma
    addresses, dates,
    greetings, closings,
      54–55
  exclamation point,
    85–87, 178, 179
  period, 82–84, 85–87,
    176, 178, 179
  question mark, 82–84,
    177, 179

Naming part of sentence,
  88–90, 171
  joining naming parts, 172

has, have, had, 153
helping verbs, 165
is, am, are, 150
names and titles of
people, 105
names of days, 111
names of holidays, 117,
120
names of months, 114
naming part of
sentence, 90
nouns, 96
nouns that show
ownership, 123
plural nouns, 99, 102
pronouns, 126
see, give, 156
sentences, 81
special animals and
places, 108
statements and
questions, 84
telling part, of
sentence, 93
verbs that tell about
now, 141
verbs that tell about the
past, 147
words that compare, 138
words that tell how
many, 135
Revising, 2, 9, 13, 17, 21, 25,
40–41

Rubrics, using, 42

S

See and *give,* 155–156, 198
Sentences
about pictures, 46–47
combining, 23
command, 85–87, 178
definition of, 79
effective, 22–25
exclamation, 85–87, 178
joining naming parts,
172
joining telling parts, 174
kinds of, 82–84, 85–87,
176, 177, 178
parts of, 88–90, 91–93,
171, 173
punctuation of, 79–81,
82–84, 85–87, 176–179
question, 82–84, 177
statement, 82–84, 176
topic sentence, 20, 49,
60–61, 64–65, 66–67
word order in, 79–81,
175
Sharing your work, 28–29
Statement. *See* **Sentences.**
Story, 52–53
personal, 50–51
Superlatives, 136–138,
191